"You're joking, right?"

My smile took a turn for the worse. "No, I am not joking."

"I'm thinking that it's wonderful! It's wonderful to have found a young woman who respects her body enough to wait for the right person. So you never even came close to doing it?"

"Not really, just light petting."

"That's all? All of this time? Honey, that's wonderful," Benjamin said, showering me with a trail of kisses across my forehead.

"Can you stop saying that it's wonderful, it's wonderful!"

"But it is, honey, don't you think so?"

"Yes I do, but don't make me out to be the Virgin Mary or anything. I'm no martyr, Benjamin." *It's wonderful, it's wonderful,* he'd stopped saying it, but I knew he was still thinking it. No doubt he was still in shock because his mouth hadn't closed all the way yet. Good thing there were no flies around.

I know, I know, don't tell me, it's wonderful right?

Shoe's on the otha' foot

HUNTER HAYES

HarperTorch
An Imprint of HarperCollins Publishers

This is a work of fiction. Names, characters, places, and incidents are products of the author's imagination or are used fictitiously and are not to be construed as real. Any resemblance to actual events, locales, organizations, or persons, living or dead, is entirely coincidental.

HARPERTORCH
An Imprint of HarperCollins*Publishers*
10 East 53rd Street
New York, New York 10022-5299

Copyright © 1998 by Hunter Hayes
ISBN: 0-06-101466-4

First HarperTorch paperback printing: September 2000

HarperCollins®, HarperTorch™, and ❦™ are trademarks of Harper-Collins Publishers Inc.

Printed in the United States of America

Visit HarperTorch on the World Wide Web at
www.harpercollins.com

     10   9   8   7   6   5

In Loving memory of my father,
Donald White,

And my cousin,
Glenn Leroy Williams

I'm missing you . . .

acknowledgments

I'd like to start out by thanking God for the way he continues to move in my life . . . unconditionally.

I'd also like to thank my mother Shirley, for believing in me even when I didn't believe in myself. I love you forever mommy.

Thanks to my dad Donald, though I miss you more than you could ever know, carrying you in my heart keeps you with me always. I love you.

Thanks to my Boogies, I couldn't have done this without the constant element of your love and support.

Brandi . . . thanks for putting your drama on hold for mine while I sat at my keyboard every day. I love you.

Thank you to Pops, a.k.a. Albert, my second dad, who I love as much as the first.

Special thanks to my agent, Denise "no-nonsense" Stinson, who's always there to help me stay on top of my toes, and my brand new editor, Carrie Feron—your patience and support have been truly instrumental to me.

I'd like to thank my entire family, the Hayes family, for being the driving force behind the source of my strength. They've encouraged me from start to finish, and it's because of them I know that I can do anything I put my mind to.

Special thanks goes out to my peoples, Kim, Michelle, Janice P. Berry (smile.), Charles Hosang you're the best, Sokoni Christian, Ayanna, Tonia, Ramona, Carol, Johanne, Cornell and Final 4, Lisa, Robin, Christine, Patricia, Pat, Latrice, Stephanie, Aunt Sandy, Mike, Eugene, Tracy R., Tracy G., Tracey at AOL, Denise, Randy, Monique, Thuraya, Anette, Etty, Errol, Rob, Hugh, Chris, Anthony, Anna Berry, Mary Flowers of Mary Flowers Entertainment, and my terrific website designer Deborah Maisonet of Webfully Yours. You're all the best.

Thanks to Black Women in Publishing and Professional Women of Color for continuing to support people like me, with dreams made into reality.

"i reminisce"

It's precisely four forty-seven p.m., and the damn beat-beat of my heart is racing to catch up with the tick-tock of my wall clock. Right. It's the beat-beat to the tick-tock. That's got me going. My mind persists in telling me that he's gonna show. *Hmph.* To be perfectly frank, sometimes I just don't want to be bothered. But then I suppose, it's normal to feel that way. I mean, it's normal for me to feel that way. One thing's for certain; I'm definitely feeling the onset of a razor-sharp attitude coming on. Reluctantly, I glance up at the wall clock, whose thin-edged hands read 4:48 p.m. *Over an hour late. Just where was he anyway?* Walking to the full-length living room mirror, I took a peek. I still looked up to par, but the feel of my palms was abnormally sweaty. I yanked a Kleenex from a nearby marbled tissue box and dried my hands. *Surely, I thought, the dampness couldn't be a physical sign of "a good thing."*

I stared long and hard at my reflection. Well, my hair was intact. Not a one of its single jet blue-black strands stood out of place. It lay parted straight down the middle and hung loosely blunt on both sides. I made a mental note to add a little something above and beyond Fifi's usual $31 fee on my next visit to the salon. She had done a hell of a job. Mouthing an "m," I gently pressed my two lips together, refreshing the layer of terra-cotta bronzed lipstick that I'd applied only twenty minutes before. I turned, strutting my stuff to get a full-body view from the sides and back. If clothes make the woman, then my two-piece mocha-colored cotton pants suit with the top that criss-crossed over my open back was working just fine for me. Just fine. I'm simply mad about natural colors and the way they look against my mapled skintone.

Confirmed. The best thing was that I hadn't looked a bit like the way I felt. For the sake of all outward appearances, I needn't have worried. I was straight. *But other things were crooked. About as crooked as the smirk I'm wearing on my face.* What was it with men anyway? Is it all that hard to figure out? Two people, working towards building a strong life-long foundation based on a trust, a love, and a mutual respect makes it just that simple. And there's absolutely nothing wrong with wanting that—not a damn thing! I guess you already know that some mystery man has me stressed to the point of no return. Oh, I'm so sorry. Allow me to introduce myself . . . I'm so rude, just rambling on and on. You don't even know who the hell I am. My name is Leslie. I'm in my early twenties. Yeah yeah, I know I'm young. *Young looking on the outside, but my soul, my soul it's old.* As old as the Mayan Civilizations in a way that keeps me independent and strong minded . . . A strong mind that tells me that from where I'm standing, I'm about to be stood up. Funny thing is, you'd think I'd have been better prepared with the way I go on.

I live alone and manage the building I live in as part of a city program that allows dumps like this one to become renovated and go co-op. My apartment's not a dump though; I put a lot of time and energy into making it resemble what I want it to be. I painted, laid down new carpeting, and furnished the place all by myself "a la Art Deco." *Martha Stewart who?* She's got nothing on me.

A college student I am, majoring in communications and working towards my Associates degree. Eventually, I'd like to be a television Producer/Writer. I've got a head full of ideas and an even stronger determination. I know I'll make it to the top. *Oh, and I'm also a virgin.* Well, I was. (I get so mixed up sometimes.) Actually, I'm not all that mixed up. It's just that my mind is always working on something. My mother swears in circles that I think too much. School, Video Production, something someone says or does . . . See, there I go doing it again. What I'm trying to tell you is that I was a virgin up until last year, around the latter part of August. Yes, I figured I was saving myself for that special man. I stand a statuesque, 5 feet 8 inches, and on a scale of 1 to 10, I'd probably rate myself about . . . a 9. As far as self-esteem goes, I've got plenty of it, and even some to share if you're lacking. I think my best feature is . . . my eyes. They're deep set and dark. I've been told that I've got bedroom eyes; I now know why, though I've never known before. There seems to be a strong element of surprise hiding behind that theory, though. Well, Surprise. I haven't had a lot of experience being in the bedroom, or anyplace else sexually for that matter.

I do feel that I'm attractive and I've never had a problem with meeting guys. I've even had a few boyfriends. They were all good looking, come to think of it, but I got out of the relationships before they could ever get serious. Anyway, I was raised by a single parent for most of my life. Namely, my mother, another strong black woman. But she always had to have a man for that financial need. Used them, abused them, and somewhere in the mix I got caught up in it all.

Physical fights with my mother and the boyfriend. Mostly, that was the biggest drama. My cries of "leave my mother alone" were in vain. I guess it sort of just came with the territory because I knew that not soon after the fight the making up would begin. And as for myself, the only child? Oh, I was sure to be compensated in some way or another. A new pet, a bright shiny blue bike with painted flowers on the seat, or even just some extra spending money. Eleven years old and walking around with $20 in my pocket on a regular basis to do as I pleased (which wasn't even counting my allowance). I know it was only my mother's guilt. As far as mom's boyfriends go, they weren't all bad. A couple were like father figures to me, even up to this very adult day. But my whole problem was, Why did she ever need those men in her life? She had me, and I loved her. She was working, what did we need them for? And what it always came back to was that physical, emotional, financial need. The men she dealt with couldn't handle that, because she wasn't giving the same thing back to them. There it is! You have to give it to get it back! So really, she's never been "in love." What she's done is given up altogether. I still pray to God she finds it. Growing up I had known early on that when I started dating, I was going to go for the full package, and not settle for anything less. I was going to get, and give the same thing in return.

I think that it goes back to values. Those good things we need to have in our lives to make us feel comfortable as a person. Friendship ranks right up there at the top for me. I've got two really good friends. Friends that I know would be there for me no matter what. There's Denise, my girl from Chicago, and then there's Rachelle. Rachelle is here with me in Manhattan, and she serves as both family member and best friend. She's my first cousin, and I couldn't imagine being here on this earth without her. I'm sure that she feels the same, and we couldn't have possibly made it through our situations without each other, as you will soon see.

So came that day, that hot-ass summer day when I was strolling home from a video-production class at my college. I didn't know it then, but that day was to become a part of my destiny, and there was virtually nothing I could do about it. It was burning up outside; it had to be at least 90 degrees, but the humidity made it feel more like 99. We had been on this heat wave tip for the past three days and I'd just about had enough of it. It was definitely gonna be a long summer, I thought as I wiped back the tiny beads of sweat which had begun to form along the base of my hairline. Fashion conscious, but burning the hell up I was, dressed in a simple white textured cotton A-line dress, and matching strappy thick-heeled sandals.

I couldn't get upstairs to my apartment soon enough to change into something cooler. Just getting buck naked would probably have been more like it. Unfortunately, before I could get there, my neighbor, who happens to also be my friend's uncle, had come up to me from across the street. He had probably seen me coming from the time I began walking down the block, since he's got nothing better to do. I knew it had to be something with my building. It was always something with my building.

"Leslie!" he called out, as he bustled up to me, practically knocking me down.

I'd almost not recognized him, without the uneven short 1975 fro that had become part of his trademark. Someone had taken time to carefully part and plait long strips of neat braid alongside his head.

"Slow down," I insisted to him. I took a step backward. If he'd a been any closer to me, we'd have kissed. The mere thought made me cringe. I didn't care if he had a new hairdo or not.

"Okay," he swallowed hard, slightly pausing to catch his breath. "The Dumpster from the city came today," he said. There was an element of excitement regenerating itself in each of his syllables. "And some men are dumping things into it!"

"Dumping things like what?" I asked, in a disgusted tone.

"I don't know," he went on. And on, and on, to give me a very detailed description of the Dumpster's contents. "Let's see, there's a short rounded table with a missing leg, eight window frames, four armchairs, two brown, one rust, one army green ... And a huge old brass floor lamp with no shade," he made sure to add, as he stared down at the broken concrete pavement beneath him.

I was glad that he was looking down at the

pavement, and not at me, because I was laughing to myself. Hadn't he just said he didn't know what they were putting in the Dumpster? "Well did you tell them that the Dumpster belonged to our building?"

"Yeah, I did, but they said they didn't see any names on it, and how it's a City Dumpster—"

"What?" I yelled, cutting him off mid-sentence. We'd waited three agonizing weeks for that damn Dumpster. We'd planned on emptying all the old furniture and debris out of apartment #19, fixing the vacant space up, and renting it out to increase our Tenants Association's monthly rent-roll collection.

"Let me go see what's going on here. Thanks," I said, as I left behind my friend's uncle, walking down the block towards the Dumpster and the guilty party at hand. Just upon reaching my destination, I spotted them. Sure enough, sure enough, two men were dumping trash from the brown bricked building directly across from our Dumpster like it was alright.

"What is it that you think you're doing here?" I asked as I walked up on them. My tone was a strong and assertive one, and my arms were folded tightly across the front of my chest. But it was like I wasn't even there with the way both men continued tossing those bags into that big metal bin.

"What does it look like?" A tall thin man slurred out from an open window. "We're using this Dumpster!"

"That's funny," I smirked. "I don't recall putting down a Mr. Skinny Man and his partner on the order for my building's Dumpster." There, that will fix 'em, I thought. "Now, I'd like to know who's in charge here."

"You're looking at him," the tall thin man said, pointing a hardened finger into his own chest.

I knew damn well that he wasn't in charge. A smarter person with any kind of authority would have had good enough sense to know better than to be sarcastic with the person who owned the Dumpster they were throwing things into.

At second glance, a short browned Dizzy Gillespie look-alike said, "That man over there, he's in charge."

As I turned to look over my shoulder, I saw another tall man, but this one was quite handsome, of medium build, kind of rugged looking. He had a smooth butterscotch complexion, the kind that you make sure to take in with the first mouthful, leaving nothing to desire on the spoon. His hair was well groomed, dark and curly, with a mustache and beard to complement. And he was coming towards me like he'd just been elected the head of the local Southern Hospitality Welcoming Committee. Caught up in that particular moment though, only left me to wonder just who this man thought he was. Had he been aware that he was using our Dumpster without any say so from anybody? Shucks, smiling and grinning the way he was at me. *Matchmaker . . . matchmaker, make me a match.* . . . I quietly hummed inside my head.

"Hello. I'm the boss, what seems to be the problem?" he'd asked me politely.

Darn, there was no melodramatic southern drawl. Somehow I'd hoped for more. "I'll say there's a problem. Who told you that you could put anything in our Dumpster!"

"I'm sorry," he apologized. "I tried to ask whose Dumpster it was, Miss. Nobody knew. So I figured why not use it? I really thought it was a City Dumpster. They order them all the time to gut out old buildings."

Oooh, he was so sincere. And informative too! I thought to myself, with fingers of mine that clenched up to form a tight fist. I wasn't gonna hit him, but I sure felt like it. "It seems to me that you didn't try asking around enough. Now what you should have done was found out whose Dumpster it really was before you figured out that you were going to start throwing things into it!" I was yelling now, unwilling and unable to maintain my composure, but he remained calm, giving me that old tired puppy-dog look that screamed out, I'm so innocent and regretful. *DAMN*. It worked. I was a lover of the four-legged breeds, and so what if he only had two. Perhaps we could work something out. It really was much too hot for this nonsense.

"I'll tell you what," I said. "I'll make a deal with you. I've got an apartment that I'm trying to empty out, so if you and your guys can help clear it, then I just might consider sharing this Dumpster with you."

His eyebrows arched up in surprise. "You've got business savvy, I see that right now. And I'll tell you what," he said as he tugged on his chin, "me and my guys will clear out the whole apartment and do anything else that you need us to do inside."

Finally, a negotiation had been reached. A sort of meeting of the minds, camaraderie at its best. I pulled together a few strands of hair from the front of my face and tucked it ever so sexily behind one of my ears. I knew I was holding the cards now. All I had to do was play my hand right, because I knew I had him right where I knew I could get him; *OPEN*.

"No, just empty out the apartment, thank you. It's apartment #19 on the fourth floor, and the elevator doesn't work. You can start now, since you've already started taking up space in my Dumpster!"

He let out a hearty laugh and I swear his eyes sparkled as he went to go get his men and start the job. I'll probably remember that moment forever . . .

I went upstairs to my top floor apartment and started doing some things. Now I don't remember what I was doing exactly, only what I was thinking. I thought, this complete stranger had just walked into my life and I couldn't stop thinking about him. I wondered if his men had finished emptying the apartment. It should have been by now, because there really wasn't all that much in there to begin with. A little "friendly investigating," that's what I'd do, I said to myself turning up the corners of my face to form a devilish smile. Besides that, I wanted to know who this man was because I didn't know a thing about him, except that he was easy on the eyes. What was his name anyway? Well, it was time to find out. I put on a new coat of lipstick and changed into my favorite Gap jeans and a short sleeve tee from Victoria's Secret, appealing yet intriguing. I didn't want this man to think I was trying to be all about him. *Because I wasn't*.

As I locked my apartment door and proceeded to walk down the stairs, I stopped to hear the muttered voices that were coming from behind the closed apartment #19. I knew one of those voices belonged to him. Now I was paranoid, wondering if he was talking about me. So I carefully leaned in pressing my ear against the door to hear whatever the heck I was gonna hear.

"No, Jimmy, move that out!" I heard a voice say.

"Man you crazy! I ain't moving no refrigerator down those stairs by myself!"

"Oh yes you are! I wanna clear everything from outta here. Let CJ help you with that!"

Mmph. Such a commanding voice. I liked that

power factor. If a man is a spineless wimp, then I don't want him. Pushing the unlocked door open slowly, I walked inside the apartment towards the voices coming from the back room.

"How's it going in here?" I asked them. He had every man in the place working, and to my surprise, almost everything completely taken out.

"Pretty good so far. Listen baby, do you want us to move that stove out too?" he asked me.

I rested the weight of my hand on my hip and replied, "First of all, let's get one thing straight. I am not your baby, so don't refer to me as that. Just give me that respect, okay?" Then he gave me that smile again, that familiar smile that let me know his response would be a real good one.

"Well you never told me your name. Maybe if I knew it, I could have called you by it. Please allow me to apologize, I'm very sorry if I offended you, and . . ."

"Leslie Williams. That's my name, now you know it!" I said abruptly, with eyes that darted all around the room.

"Okay, I'll address you as Ms. Williams," he tells me.

He was being fuckin sarcastic, but I was loving every minute of this conversation. I can't really say what it was. Maybe it was the play on words, or the battle of wits, or maybe it was just the way his lips moved when he spoke. For some odd reason, my eyes were transfixed there.

"Leslie will be fine, just fine," I told him. I didn't want to be too mean to him because after all, I felt drawn to this person in a strange way that I'd never felt before. While he shoveled debris from the kitchen, I acted like I was looking around the apartment, but I was really watching him.

"You know that's a coincidence. I had a girl-friend in California with your name," he said from out of nowhere.

Well who the hell had asked him all that? He wanted to know my name and I told him. *Who me? Jealous? Hmph*.

I managed to let out a very monotone:

"Oh really?"

"Yep," he said.

Yep? What the fuck was a yep? Was that all he could say? By now I'd had my fill of this man. All I wanted to do was go back upstairs to my apart-ment and have an ice cold drink, and maybe a slice of that peach cobbler I had stood on line for 15 minutes at Wimps Bakery for the day before. So I walked out. I walked all the way out of the room, down the hall, and straight out of the front door remembering to yell out an, "Oh yeah, and you can get rid of that stove too!"

Damn. I hated myself for wolfing down those two helpings of cobbler and that large glass of ice tea. I rubbed my stomach. I was really upset, but I didn't know why. It had also just dawned on me that I still hadn't found out what this man's name was. I decided to give my friend Patrice a call to see how she was doing. Patrice is . . . to describe in a few words . . . simply, UNPREDICTABLE. She lives by the motto "do as I say, not as I do." It is for this very reason that I try to avoid telling her any of my personal business, because she is highly analytical, and too damn critical. Still, I always wind up opening up my big mouth. It's like the words just bust out with no damn warning. This time would be different though. This time I promised not to talk about myself, but about any, and everybody, else.

"Hey girl, what's up?" I asked.

"Who is this?"

"Who the hell do you think it is? It's me, Leslie."

"Ohh . . . whatsup?" Patrice answered upon second realization.

"Nothing much. I just finished stuffing my face," I told her as I undid the top button on my jeans. Good, at least I could breathe now. I'd take it easy on the peach cobbler the next time around.

"Man problems, huh?" Patrice asked. The question born to be a statement undoubtedly. It was, basically, all I had to say. "Well there's no problem on this end. Girl, let me tell you," Patrice went on, "I met this guy, he's got it going on! The body on this guy is like booming! Well, I went to his house . . . Honey, one thing led to another, and. . . ."

Somewhere in between the story I had to tune

Patrice out. In fact, I'd had enough time to actually contemplate wrapping my spiraled telephone cord around my neck. It was the same-o-same-o. She met a new man, he looked good, probably didn't have too much going on for himself, but she just had to fuck him. Ecetera, Ecetera . . .

"Leslie, are you still there? Girl you haven't been listening to a word I've been saying," Patrice said in her usual high pitched voice. It was the voice she was destined to squeak out for the rest of her natural born life. A voice, nonetheless, that I had grown to get used to throughout our eight-year since-we-were-kids friendship.

"Yes I have been listening. It's just that I've had so much on my mind lately. Girl, I just don't know sometimes . . . ," I said.

"Talk to me Leslie."

Here I go again, me and my big assed mouth. **I could have kicked myself. Hard.**"Well," I began, "I met this guy today, actually he's a man. I don't even know his name. He's older though, very good looking, and I think he's into real estate, or contracting or something."

"Yeah, and?"

"Yeah, and that's it, that's just it. There is no more. But I find myself somehow feeling kind of drawn to him."

"You are?" Patrice's squeaky voice went down an octave, a tell tale sign of trouble. "Well, how old is he?"

"He looks to be about thirty-something."

"Hmph," Patrice muffled under her breath.

Then I think to myself, oh great, here comes the stupid advice.

"Honey, watch out for those older men, you're only twenty-something and he's thirty-something. He's more experienced, he might try to take advantage of you! I don't want to see you get hurt. Girl . . . that's a messed up feeling," Patrice said with a heavy high sigh. I was just thankful that we didn't have to go back to her first-love/first-hurt story.

"Patrice, I am not stupid. I know how to handle my own relationships."

"What relationships?" Patrice asked me sarcastically, "you've never had a real one. For God sakes girl, you're still a virgin, and at your age! He'll have to blow it open with a time bomb!" She chuckled. "Take it from me, you still gotta lot to learn!"

Then I think, time to tune Patrice out again. I love her, but what kind of person was she to talk? All of her relationships were dead, and I sure-nuff didn't see her with no Mr. Right. And another damn thing, we're the same age, I grew up with the girl, and I'm just a little sorry about that, because maybe then she wouldn't have known that I was a virgin. Always rubbin shit in. (No pun intended.) Don't get me wrong, I don't feel bad about having been one, but I don't need anyone to throw that virgin shit in my face like it is *"THEEE"* ultimate sign of maturity. I pressed a button on my cordless telephone to resemble the sound of a click as though it was my call waiting, because I could see that this conversation was going nowhere fast.

"Oh that's my other line girl, let me see who this is. Are you going to be home? It's probably my mother, let me call you back."

"Well no, I'm not going to be here," Patrice said. "I've got a date with that cutie I was tellin you about, but I'll give you a call tomorrow to let you know how it went."

"Can't wait," I said, lying. The things we do and say in the name of friendship, I thought to myself. "Alright now, don't do anything I wouldn't do!" I said.

"Are you trying to depress me? I do want to have some fun tonight."

"Ha, ha, ha," I said, and with that I hung up the phone.

I lay down on my Italian custom rust colored leather couch with the stereo on. The sounds of the brown sugar babied D'Angelo floated in the background, drifting me off to sleep. Well the brother must have helped me into bed sometime during the middle of the night. I woke up in my bed the next day, checking the time on my nightstand. 9:30 a.m. It was still dark outside, and the absence of the sun's usual bright presence in my bedroom led me to think that it was earlier than it really was. It looked like rain, all clouds and no sun. Time for me to raise up and haul myself off to class.

I was going to be late again. My history class

was scheduled to start at 10:00 and I knew I wouldn't reach school until at least 10:30. Why didn't I remember to set the alarm? School was the place to be. School was the place where I would get my damn degree, so that I could get on with my life, and do what I had to do. That's just how I saw it. I showered and slipped into my favorite summer dress, added shoes, a quick touch of lipstick and earthtone eye shadow, grabbed my bag, and dashed out the door on my way to class.

❖

Bang, clack, clutter, bang, bang, clack, clutter, almost a tool quartet. Those were the sounds I heard coming from across the street from the building "He" was working in. I decided to walk really fast, pretending not to hear or see him. A sure way of keeping things uncomplicated. I passed each building as though it were a hurdle. So far so good. Maybe he doesn't see me, I said to myself, seemingly unnoticed. Passing each building I began to count one . . . two . . . three . . . four . . .

"Leslie!" he called out. . . .

◆ **2**

taking chances

As I quickened my pace, I could hear the sounds of footsteps fast approaching from behind me where the voice was calling. The next thing I knew, I was turning around to feel the gentle grip of someone tugging on the back of my arm.

"Didn't you hear me calling you?" he asked.

I gave him one of my best I'm-mean-so-don't-bother-me looks and kept walking, taking up long even strides, putting a good distance between us. From the very corner of my eye, I could see him. He was doing well keeping up with my pace, not lagging far behind. I refused to turn around and look at him directly. He had on one of those one-piece, I don't know what you call it, I guess blue-jean farmer-brown kind of overall numbers, a crisp white tee-shirt, and some brown Timberland work boots. His hair was cut in a fade, low and contoured on the sides, and a muss of natural black curls on top that seemed to almost glisten beneath the sun. His beard was shaped in what some ladies call the five-o-clock shadow. In other words, it was shaped right.

"Leslie, I'm talking to you, didn't you hear me calling you?" he asked again, this time smiling, because now he was onto my game, or so I thought.

"Yes, I heard you calling me. Frankly, I wish that you wouldn't."

"Why?" he asked, with a smile that widened out to meet mine.

"What's with all the questions? You writing a book? Do me a favor, stop calling my name out in the street Mr. Slickster." (That one just came to me).

"What? Oh, so now I'm Mr. Slickster. Why would you call me a name like that?" he asked.

"Because you're slick, that's why," I said, turning to finally look him in the face. "There's just something about you . . . Oh never mind!" I told him, shifting my gaze back to the straight-ahead mode.

Before I realized where I really was, I was there. We were at the train station, and *he* had walked me all the way.

"Listen Leslie, you got a telephone? I'd like to

have your number. Maybe I can give you a call sometime."

"No I don't, but you're free to give me your number. That is, if you want to," I added. He didn't have to.

"You don't have a telephone," he replied in a cynical voice. "Okay-fine, we'll do this your way." He took out a small stack of business cards from his back jean pocket and handed one to me.

"Is this your home phone number? I ask because I don't like beepers, not unless it's business," I said.

"Well, there is a lot of work to be done in your building. I can do the job, you know. Did you like how I cleaned out the apartment?"

"Yes, and I bet you could do the job, but unfortunately, I don't have any control over who gets hired to do the work in my building," I said with a straight face. It wasn't a total lie. Any work done in my building required a sign off by at least two officers to a check. I'm one. One of the major officers who signs the checks.

"Well then, I guess it doesn't matter either way, because it's not a beeper number, Ms. Smarty." He pointed to two different telephone numbers. "This is my work number, and the other one is my home number."

I started to walk down into the subway station, when I heard him calling me from the top of the stairs.

"Leslie! I almost forgot to tell you, my name is

Benjamin, and it's social. I'm almost positive that you already know that though."

I smiled. "Have a nice day Mr. Slickster." I laughed and he shook his head and smiled back. Yes, there was a whole lot of smiling going on.

Sitting on the train on the way downtown, I looked around as I always do, at the people around me. I guess you could call it force of habit, with me being a native New Yorker and all. There was no one out of the ordinary except for this one woman who was trying to apply thickened black mascara onto her eyelashes in the steadily moving car. I hoped the train would stop short and make her look like a raccoon. It would serve her right. I hated the rush of the city. I tried to think calming thoughts and found myself looking down at the textured black and white business card that I held in my hand. Hmm . . . Benjamin. Nice name, very appropriate. Well at least he had a name now. I chuckled to myself about the whole little episode with him. I had the telephone number now, work and home. I was liking the way things were working out. I read on, Bailey and Rabinowitz: General Contractors. One of the names sounded Jewish, that couldn't be his, that must be his partner. Benjamin Bailey. That was his, and it was nice. *Leslie Bailey*. Nice ring. Pairing his last name with mine already? Clearly, I was losing my mind. I put the card away and took my Video Production book from out of my bag, reviewing the chapters Professor Ivers had assigned for us to read. By the time I looked up from my book, I had reached my destination.

As I passed the guys standing around in front of the college, they called out,

"Hey Miss, can I talk to you for a minute?"

"That's a pretty outfit you got on."

Blah, blah, blah, in one ear, and out the other. All of the guys at my college were the same way, very into themselves, and wanting very much to be into you, and every other female in the place. Experience makes me an expert, so you don't just think I'm making this up. Let's see . . . first there was Khalif, a real cutie. He's mixed with something, fine as hell, and not conceited. All I visioned was a very good looking young man with a major, a sense of direction, and a part time job. Khalif's problem? I can't really say that there was one because the attraction was there for both of us, but we just never clicked. Besides that, he moved out of state, so I deemed the relationship to be "virtually impossible," and a "just wasn't meant to be." Then there was Jay, the handsome type, a real go-getter. He knew exactly what he wanted out of life, but somehow, the relationship thing was at the bottom of the list. And get this, he expected me to wait around! *I don't think so.* Erick, Wendell, Tyrone, and Lance are a few more of the losers who can contribute to the reason why I don't talk to guys at my college. So when I pass those stupid guys who stand in front of the school, it's not because I'm trying to be cute, or that I think I'm all that, it's just because I have my reasons.

Class was over in no time, probably due to the fact that I was so late. There was only so much one could learn in 25 minutes.

I headed back home for a 1:30 meeting with a coordinator from TIL (Tenants Interim Lease) regarding some building repairs. As I reached the fifth floor of my building, I could hear the sound of my phone ringing on the upper level above. I sprinted up the remaining flight to catch it thinking it might be TIL people calling to cancel. I didn't feel like wasting my day waiting to be stood up.

"Hello," I said breathing heavily collapsing onto the sofa.

"Hey Ms., long time no speak," the voice on the other line said.

"Who is this?" I asked.

"It's me."

My first guess might have been Benjamin, but it really didn't sound like him, and I knew that I didn't give him my definitely unlisted telephone number.

"I don't feel like playing games, so either tell me who you are, or you get the dial tone."

"Well since you put it that way, whatsuuup!, it's Errol!"

I let out a loud whatsuuup right back at him. I was so happy to be hearing from my friend. I hadn't heard from him in about four months.

Errol used to go to my college. He's a natural flirt and born womanizer at heart, but I don't hold it against him because of the level that our friendship has progressed to. He's never tried to push up on me or make any moves, so he gets all of my respect. Errol is and will always be like the little brother I've never had, being that he's only a year younger than I am.

"So what have you been up to?" I asked him.

He told me that he had traveled to the Bahamas to visit some family. I was glad to learn that he's living in Florida, employed with a good job at a pharmaceutical company. Lastly, and probably the most astonishing of all, was how he was thinking about getting married.

"You? Married?" I asked. "You're joking right? You mean to tell me that you're going to give up all those females you're dealing with for just one? I thought variety was your spice of life!"

"Believe it Leslie, I'm telling you. All of those other females are cut off. You're listening to a man in love. I just got turned off from playing all of those head games, and especially nowadays with AIDS and all that other shit out there, it's just not worth it," Errol told me.

"Well who is she? Who is this woman who has single-handedly managed to capture your heart?" I asked.

"Her name is Monique, and she's twenty-two. She's a beauty," he added.

Why was I getting a mental picture of a young

buxom woman with big bumper lights? I continued to listen, in all fairness to him.

"She goes to school for business administration, and works at a bank. I can't explain it, but she's just different from those other females I've dealt with in the past."

"Damn Errol, if I didn't hear you saying it, I wouldn't believe it. But marriage? Don't you think that's a little extreme?"

"No I don't, she's the one."

"Errol I've heard you say that a few times before," I said, remembering a time not too long ago. "I think her name was Angie, and before that, Jerlette."

"Baby I'm for real . . ." Errol began to sing out in a chorus of song.

"Okay, okay," I laughed, "you're still crazy!"

"And what about you, Ms. Leslie, how's school, how's your building, and what's been going on in your love life? You still breaking hearts?"

"School's fine, the building is coming along, and my love life is dead."

"What! Not you with a dead love life!"

"Yes it is dead Errol, there's nobody out there for me."

"Maybe you're just looking too hard."

"That's just it, I'm not looking at all!" My thoughts immediately went to Benjamin. I decided not to mention him in this conversation, it was way too premature.

"Well then that's the problem. Maybe if you showed a little more interest in someone, and stopped being so mean and anti-social, you could meet somebody."

"Thank you for trying to build up my spirit Mr. Oprah, I'll give it some thought," I laughed. "And don't forget to send me an invitation to the wedding."

"Don't you know? You're unforgettable," Errol said. "Now you take care, and more importantly, take my advice."

"I will," I answered. I'll take care. I don't know about that advice part, I thought. Imagine, me anti-social? "I don't think so," I said to my telephone, only after I had hung up the receiver.

❖

1:45 and still no TIL, so I go downstairs to meet the coordinator in front of the building. As usual, there was something going on everywhere, with the excitement of summer buzzing all around. Little girls playing jump rope across the street, little boys running and leaping, a few drug dealers. Yes I know, can't forget the drug dealers. For the love of money . . . that's the song that comes to mind every time I think about it. Neighbors gossiping and the loud bass of the music resounding from the passing cars and Jeeps. It's sometimes enough to make you crazy, but it's where I live now, so I'm making the most of it. But even with everything going on good and bad, it's my community, and I feel connected. It's home base, and no matter where I go, part of it will go with me. Personally, I think that this new city program is one of the best things that ever happened to me, to these people, even though they don't know it yet. We may have the chance to own our own apartments. It'll be something to call our own.

As I glance up the block, I finally see our TIL Building Coordinator, Elaine Bishop, heading towards me. She's really a wonderful person fighting hard to keep our building in the TIL Program.

"Sorry I'm so late, but the Uptown trains were all messed up," she said. "There was a sick passenger in one of the cars."

I wondered how much money she made. She was so stylish. Always with a patterned scarf, or shades and a matching purse. I hoped it was a sign that she was being paid her worth. I wouldn't wish her job on anyone. Motivate, push, motivate, push, but follow the TIL guidelines. It was always that.

"It's okay, I got caught up talking to an old friend anyway," I told her, as we walked up the stairs towards my apartment. My neighbors gave us looks that could kill, huddled in their little cliques of twos and threes whispering on the steps of the adjoining brownstone buildings that stood next to mine. I was so tired of that crap. When were they going to realize that I wasn't the

fuckin' landlord? When were they going to realize that we're all in this thing together? When
were they going to realize that this is not a con-
spiracy against them from me and the employees
of TIL?

Our coordinator gave me a sympathetic look
and a pat on the back. I guess that was supposed
to mean something. Take some advice from me,
never work where you live, because your life will
never be your own. My thing is to set this program off, to see it happen and move on, to prove
to these damn people that we can definitely
accomplish something if we persevere.

At the end of our very extensive two-hour
meeting, I walked our coordinator downstairs.
The meeting was nothing new. In fact, everything that the coordinator was telling me, I
already knew.

"You need to form committees. Tenant repair,
rent collections, and maintenance, and hold more
regular meetings," she'd say.

The problem was that we just had to get those
wheels turning. Same song, different day, I
thought. "Thanks for coming out," I'd said waving a five fingered good-bye to Elaine. I was glad
that the meeting was over.

I don't know why I did it, but I looked across the
street to see Benjamin unloading some sheet rock

from a large blue Ford truck. He must have just rode up, because I hadn't noticed the truck there before. He hadn't seen me, but I knew I wanted to be seen. Instead, I went on about my business to the Chinese restaurant to get some take-out. No way was I cooking tonight. I'd just turned the corner of my block when I noticed that all of the sheet rock that was once on the truck was now gone, and so was Benjamin. This was ridiculous. I was letting this man monopolize too many of my thoughts. I returned to my apartment and greedily devoured my chicken and fried rice, and then decided to do some reading. *Petals In The Valley* was the new book I'd started. It was starting to get good, and I wanted to finish it, so I read:

Kurt slowly unbuttoned her blouse, and tenderly cupped her firm rounded breasts, first in his hands . . . then into the fiery center of his mouth . . .

"Damn!" I yelled, throwing the book down onto the floor. The book was a little too good.

I walked over to the window looking down at the front street, when I saw *him* sitting on the steps of the building he worked in. I quickly moved back from the window pulling the curtains closed. *I didn't want to see him, I wanted to see him,* so I moved over to the other window in my bedroom. This particular window had mini-blinds that I could easily look through undetected. So I slowly but carefully parted the mini-blinds and peeped out. Was he just tired? He just sat there while the activity of the other men moved along around him. Perhaps he was waiting for someone, I thought. He suddenly looked up to my window. I drew back immediately, closing my eyes, somehow believing that once I re-opened them I could make it go away. Had he seen me there all along? Maybe he was looking at a passing plane. Coming to grips with reality I then realized that I was the one peeking on him. *Ha! I was a stalker!* What was I doing? I moved back so quickly from that window . . . I swear he looked up! How did he know where I lived? Sleep. I needed some sleep. That was the only excuse I could come up with for my damn behavior. Never in my life had I liked someone I knew so little about, in so little time.

※ **3**

brotherly love

Two whole weeks. Two whole weeks was how long I would be out of town and the timing couldn't be better. Classes were out on account of holiday, and I really needed the break. Hope sprung eternal in my search to find a little peace of mind. I was on my way to Philadelphia, Pennsylvania, to stay with my good high school friend Denise. Denise is crazy cool. She's married to Darryl, her very away a lot husband, who works for the Federal government. They've been married for two years now, and seem to have the ideal relationship. It probably has something to do with the fact that he's away most of the time. When he comes home they miss each other so much that there's little room for arguments, and those trivial things that most married people go through. Denise is a down to earth type of person anyway, marriage or no marriage, and so is Darryl. I guess that's why it works for them.

My train pulled into the station at 2:00 p.m. Denise told me that she would be picking me up at around 2:30, so you know what that meant. I'd have to wait a whole thirty minutes until she came. No problem, I thought to myself, there's some gift shops in the station that I wouldn't mind checking out. You know how people are, when you go out of town, they always want you to bring shit back for them.

The first shop that I went into had some zany colored Philly T-shirts in the window, so I went in to purchase a few. I'd get one for my mom, one for Patrice and Cuz, and one for myself. I looked through the racks searching for another extra-large tee, but I couldn't seem to find one. Small, small, medium, medium, small. Where was a salesperson when you needed one? I went over to the cash register and yelled out to the back. Maybe they had some in stock somewhere. A scruffy guy from the back came out and told me that they didn't. Well I wasn't really looking where I was going, still looking around the store to see what else they had, and somehow or another, I wound up bumping into this very tall, very handsome stranger. He was what I call the chocolate man. At what looked to be about 6'3" he stood, with skin as smooth as lotion, a deep, dark bald head, and a set of the most succulent lips you've ever seen.

"Oh excuse me," I said. "I was . . ." I started to say, before I took in the masculine scent of Drakar on his shirt.

"No, please allow me to apologize. It was my fault. I should have been looking where I was going. Are you alright?" he asked me.

Was I alright? Was a green pea green? Mmhmm. I was real good now.

"Yes, I'm fine. It was probably my fault, you see I was looking for this tee-shirt, extra large, to sleep in, and they didn't have any left in my size . . ."

"Extra-large! Get outta here!" He exclaimed, showing genuine interest in every word that I'd said. I suddenly realized that I'd been rambling again, and he must have realized it too because we both started to laugh. Uncontrollably, to the point where other people in the store were looking at us.

"Could we get a little help over here, since everyone in this store seems to be so interested in what we're doing!" he said. Quicker than a speeding bullet, this man had managed to get a salesperson, and solve my little problem. Turns out that they'd just gotten in a new shipment of even better tee-shirts. And guess what? They had all sizes. **Go figure**.

As I got handed my shopping bag full of tee-shirts, all I could muster was a warm smile, and an even warmer, "Thank you."

"You're very welcome," he said, giving me a smile back. "I'm Rob, and you are?"

"Leslie."

"You're beautiful Leslie," he said.

"Excuse me?" I asked him.

"I said, you're beautiful."

"Thanks, the flattery will get you everywhere," I said to him. The fact that he had been such a help to me in the shop had been working in his favor, amongst other things.

"Maybe even dinner?" he asked.

"Maybe, dinner . . ."

Having had only a half hour to spare, I knew that Denise was probably looking for me.

"Do you have the time Rob?"

"It's . . . 2:45."

"Oh my goodness! Let me get outta here!" We were already walking up to the waiting area in the station. I saw Denise from the distance, yelled out her name, and gave a big wave once she spotted me. Rob handed me a card with his name and phone number on it and told me to call him when I was ready to go out. Oh, and he kissed my hand too. Who said chivalry was dead? Denise and I ran towards one another with our arms flung open.

"Look what time it is girl! Can you please explain how it turned out that your train is here, but you're fifteen minutes late? And, can you also please tell me how you can be here for only fifteen of those late minutes, and have that fine-assed man you met drooling all over you?"

"I don't know girl, just lucky?" I replied, blushing.

We laughed and reminisced all the way to the baggage pick-up and to the car. Denise looked good as always. Her hair had grown even longer than the last time I had seen her, it grew way past her shoulders and she was dressed in a very relaxed way, sporting tennis shoes, khakis and a ribbed white tee-shirt. She looked like she'd just stepped off a page out of the J Crew catalogue. She'd lost a good amount of weight and it looked great on her.

"So how's my brother-in-law doing?" I asked her on the ride home as I looked out the window at the passing scenery. I marveled at the part of Philly that we were driving through. It resembled New York.

"He's good, right now he's in Chicago," Denise replied.

"Whaaat, Denise how do you do it? I mean, how do you make it with Darryl being away so much? Don't you miss him?"

"Yeah girl, but we talk to each other on the phone like every night."

"But that can't be the same," I said.

"No it's not the same, Darryl and I do something that most couples don't do."

"What? New sexual positions?"

"No crazy! We communicate, you know, we keep the lines open. Darryl does that, and a lot of men won't. Maybe they feel like it's too much emotion for them to show or something! But we're happy. The biggest problem is that Darryl's a neat freak and I'm a slob! Girl, when he comes home that house is in such a mess!"

We laughed, and laughed, and laughed some more.

"Well I sure hope you cleaned up for my visit because I'm on vacation, and I ain't doing a thing!"

"No girl, you won't have to. I straightened up some," Niece joked.

"Well here we are, home sweet home!" We pulled into the circular driveway of Denise's house. I hadn't been out to visit her in a year, and they had remodeled the house since the last time I came out. Everything was totally different from what I had remembered.

"You go girl!" The house was on. It was like an ultra-modern design, mauve and charcoal gray if you can picture it. I could only imagine what the inside looked like. Besides the fact that Denise's husband works for the Federal government, Denise holds down a position as a self-employed financial consultant. Success is no stranger to the Spencer household. When we finally got all of my one hundred and one bags from out of the trunk of the car and into the house, Denise and I plopped down onto her large black and white pinstriped chaise couch, exhausted and hungry.

"I love what you've done with the place girl! It must have cost you a small fortune!" I told her.

"Thanks girl."

"Yes, I love what you've done with everything," I said, getting up and looking around. It was kind of messy, but I visualized it as spotless. Denise was a slob and there was no denying that. "I'm starving, what do you have around this place to eat?" I was in the kitchen now, and had to yell out for her to hear me. When I opened the refrigerator door, I was very disappointed, to say the least. All Denise had in the refrigerator was health food. Health food to the left of me, health food to the right of me. Tofu, lettuce, non-fat plain yogurt, rice-cakes, and bottled water. There must have been at least a dozen or so large containers of it. "Denise!" I yelled out. "What are you trying to do, starve yourself? Girl, we have got to go shopping! We gotta get some real food in this house!"

"Child, I don't eat that junk any more," Denise replied. "I cut all of that crap right out! Do you know how many calories there is in all of that fatty, greasy food that you eat?" Denise asked.

"Frankly my dear, I don't give a damn!" I exclaimed, "Give me fat! Give me calories! Feed me! That's what I'm talking about!"

"Well I'm talking about really looking and feeling good about yourself. Don't you see all the weight I lost? We're not getting any younger, you know, and watching what we eat is important, you gotta take care of your body. You've only got one," Denise said.

"Okay," I told her, "we'll compromise. I'll eat a little of your health food and you'll eat a little of my not-so-healthy food, just for old times sake. Come on Denise, remember how we used to throw down in High School? You remember crabs, burgers, Chinese food, Soul food. . . . We used to go all out, remember?"

"Well . . . I know I'll hate myself later for agreeing to this, but . . . alright! You'll never change, you always get your way with everything. Next stop, the supermarket!" Denise chimed in.

◆

We really racked up, that "just a little bit" turned into a whole lot. We bought tacos, cold cuts, ingredients for fried chicken, baked macaroni and cheese, and for dessert, banana pudding. Denise and I cooked it up, and the next thing we knew, we were stuffing our faces.

"Just like old times!" Denise said in between chicken bites.

"Yeah, I just hope that I don't get sick," I said, "maybe this wasn't the best idea."

"All of this food tastes so good to me! I'll be working this stuff off way after you leave for sure!" Denise replied, greedily. Now instead of chicken it was the banana pudding, and she had the nerve to top it off with a scoop of vanilla ice-cream!

After eating, we decided to go into the living room to watch some old videos of Darryl on his trips. Denise has gone along on many of his travels. She can't go with Darryl on that many assignments anymore because her business keeps her very busy at home for much of the time.

"And this is Darryl and me, at the Grand Canyon in Colorada. . . . and this is Darryl acting like he's going to jump off the cliff, and. . . . ."

It must have been at least the fourth video we'd watched, and I was starting to experience a case of home-video overdose. I thought it would never end, the tapes were so extraordinarily long. Denise was acting as though she'd never seen the damn tapes before in her life, all giddy and shit.

"And this is me by the cliff," Denise continued.

"Do you think I should call him?" I'd asked her.

"Call who?" Denise asked me back, in an almost angry tone, probably because I'd interrupted her in the middle of one of her rare video moments.

"You know, the guy I met at the train station! He gave me his telephone number! You know Rob!" I said.

"You mean that fine hunk of a chocolate man about 6'2", dark brown bedroom eyes, chisel-chinned man with the dimple on his left cheek?"

"Yes! I believe that's him alright. Damn girl! Seems like I should watch out for you," I laughed. "You might try to push up on him for yourself!"

"No thank you Ms. Leslie," Denise said. "He's not quite my type. I prefer the neater more neurotic types," Denise replied.

"You never know," I said. "He might just be messy, and extremely neurotic! I think that everybody is neurotic to some degree."

"Leslie, just go ahead and call him, there's only one way to really find out if he is or isn't!" Denise urged.

"You're right," I said, "I'll call him." Denise came over to the telephone where I was and leaned a close ear in on the upcoming conversation. We were both smiling from ear to ear. I dialed the number written on the card. It was ringing, why was I even calling him? I felt like hanging up. I felt like I was back in High School again. Should I hang up? I thought to myself. Just as I'd decided to, I got,

"Hello," the voice said on the end of the other line. I was like a teenager all scared to speak.

"Hello Rob, it's Leslie."

"Oh hi!" Rob replied in a cheery voice.

I took that as a sign that he was happy to hear from me.

"I didn't expect to hear from you for a while," he said.

"Why?" I asked.

"Because you seem like the type that has to give a man a hard time, so that he knows what he has," Rob said.

"And what would you have if you had me?" I asked playfully; suddenly I wasn't so scared to speak.

"All I'd ever need," he answered.

Denise nudged me in the back with her elbow, causing me to laugh.

"Good answer, I like that."

"What's he saying?" Denise nudged me again.

"Shhh!" I told her.

"Hello?" Rob said.

"Yeah I'm here, there's something going on with this stupid phone!" I said.

"So when can I see you?" Rob asked me.

"When would you like to see me?"

"What about tonight, around sevenish?"

"Go Leslie! Go Leslie!" Denise cheered quietly in the background.

"Okay, you can pick me up at . . ."

"224 Shepard Lane," Denise whispered to me.

"224 Shepard Lane," I repeated. "It's the gray house in the middle of the block. You can't miss it! See you then!"

"Alright" he said. Click. The deed had been done.

"Girl, what you wearin?" Denise asked me, as she gave me a giant hug. I couldn't tell who was more excited, her or me.

By seven-fifteen, the doorbell was ringing and I was just about ready-to-go. I opted for a two-piece navy lycra-spandex pant suit with brush gold accessories, and just for a change, I wore my hair in a sexy upsweep. You couldn't tell me nothing. I just hoped this Rob guy was worth it. I was applying a coat of natural mocha matte lipstick, when Denise came up the stairs rushing into the bathroom.

"Girl he's here! Hurry up! Don't keep that fine man waiting too long! You look good, now go ahead!"

"How does he look?" I asked.

Denise transformed her face up in an uptight manner and mouthed the words, "I-Said-He-Looks-Fine!"

I laughed and went downstairs to greet my date, with Denise pulling in the rear.

"You look wonderful," Rob said to me as I came down the stairs.

"And so do you," I said back to him. I really did mean it because the brother looked GOOD. He was dressed in a three-piece silk suit, sandy beigish color, and some black Italian shoes to match. I was impressed.

"Well you two have a good time, and it was very nice meeting you Rob."

"You too Denise. Maybe we can all go out when your husband comes back in town."

"That sounds good, right Leslie?"

"Oh yeah, sounds good, real good!" I said, even though I knew I was only in town for this week. But Rob didn't have to know that now.

Rob opened the door as we finished saying our Goodnights to Denise, and I happened to look over by the curb, only to see the blinding shine of the Acura Legend Coupe sitting by the curb. This man had taste.

"My car's parked right out front," Rob said.

Call me psychic. I wondered if Dionne Warwick had any openings in The Network. We walked over to the car and Rob ran over to the passenger side to open the door for me.

"Thank you," I said. Now don't go assuming things about me because I'm no gold-digger. I can do for myself. I'm used to good things, and the fact that Rob has a nice appearance and a nice car is only a plus. Rob got into the driver's seat and slipped in a Branford Marsalis CD. I knew it was Branford, because I'm a big Marsalis fan, I've got the same CD at home.

"I love Branford Marsalis' music. It's so mellow," I told him.

"You know Branford's supposed to be coming this way in a couple of weeks. He'll be at this jazz bar that a good friend of mine owns. I'm sure that I could get us a couple of tickets, if you want to go," Rob said.

"I'd like that," I said. "But to tell the truth, I'm only here visiting from New York. I might be able to try and get back down though. Who was I kidding? I knew I'd never be able to get back here in a couple of weeks from now, but if things continued to go as good as it was going, I'd sure try my best. We started the evening off by getting something to eat, my favorite pastime.

We went to this very nice seafood place that Rob knew of. It overlooked the harbor. I got my eat on, as usual, not even trying to play cute finishing my meal of baked red snapper, and almost half of Rob's king crab legs. Good conversation made dinner real cozy. Rob opened up and told me about his ex-girlfriend and how she had played him for a fool. Right then I knew that I'd have to take it extra slow with this one, because there was nothing worse than a man scorned. They never forget that shit. But then I thought to myself, maybe this one is different, and it can't hurt to give him the benefit of the doubt. Then I thought, I think too much. I was just going to enjoy the rest of the evening.

Our next destination was the jazz club. We went to the one that Rob's friend owns. Shazz, that was the name of it, and it was bad. The whole atmosphere was so cool and relaxing. Pictures of jazz greats hung along the walls. Dizzy Gillespie, Miles Davis, and the like. The live jazz band played cool melodies over the swaying couples on the dance floor. The moment we stepped into the club, people were all over Rob. Women and men.

"Hey Rob, long time no see," a sultry red-headed female said, mouthing a puckered kiss to Rob. What was her problem? Didn't she see me with the man? Respect amongst sisters and brothers, that's what I'm talkin about. But I wasn't going to let her get to me, I'm secure within myself, forget all of that petty stuff. The men who spoke to Rob eyed me up and down like I was up for sale or something. I guess they liked what they saw, and so did Rob because he tightened his hand grip around my waist, as in a "this is mine" manner. We grabbed a candlelit table in the far corner and Rob ordered us something to drink.

"Wanna dance?" Rob asked.

"Why not?" I answered. We danced like two star-crossed lovers. I was having such a good time, happy that I'd decided to take the trip, and the date. We were dancing really close, so close that I could feel the bulge growing in Rob's midsection. I could tell he was well endowed. He was teasing me, because somewhere in between getting lost in my thoughts, and the dancing, Rob had begun to press his manhood harder against my leg. His firm flesh was against mine. It felt alright, I must admit. Then, taking things a step further, he started to gyrate. Okay, I thought, but I didn't say anything. Then, he moved his hands off my waist onto my butt, and started squeezing real hard. He wouldn't let go.

"Rob, let go." I said in a calm voice. "Let's stop dancing now. Did you hear me? Let go," I said once again, in a lower stern voice, trying not to make a scene.

"Come on now!" he said. "We're just dancing, having a good time!"

And still, he hadn't let go. In fact, he was holding me closer and squeezing me tighter. He was making a spectacle of both of us, and he wasn't even drunk. So I did what I had to do. I slowly raised my right knee, giving him a sharp one in the groin.

"Oohh!" he hollered out in pain. "What's wrong with you! You crazy or something!"

I walked across the dance floor, over to the table without him.

"Grow up Leslie!" He yelled over at me. "This is the nineties, get with it! I mean what did you expect me to do Miss Lady, you weren't complaining before. There are plenty of women in here who would be more than happy to dance with me. I look good, I got a good job, I drive a nice car. You better watch what you're walking away from!" he added, walking over to the table and pulling out his chair to sit.

"Seems as if everywhere we go, we draw attention," I said. I got up, grabbed my handbag, wrapped my scarf around my neck and added, "In answer to your question Rob, what I expected was to get a little respect. Seems that's something you can't show for one whole night!"

"Save it sweetheart!" he replied, taking a drink and holding his crotch.

Save it I did, I wasn't going to waste any more breath on this man, so I left. I didn't bother to look back.

I waved down a yellow cab, and when I got home, I remembered that I didn't have a key. Ringing the doorbell would wake Denise up. It was something I didn't want, because it meant that I'd have to tell her how my night went. With no choice I rang. A very groggy Denise unlocked and opened the door.

"Hey," Denise said drowsily. Good, I thought, she was out of it, maybe she wouldn't ask me anything.

"How was tonight? Where's Rob? Didn't he

drive you home?" Denise asked looking around for Rob or his car.

"Awful. Who knows? And no!, to answer all three of your questions! On top of that, I'm tired, I'm going to bed, and goodnight!" I went upstairs to my room, slamming the door behind me.

"Goodnight to you too!" Denise yelled out.

I laughed. Nothing like a good friend to make you laugh when you're feeling down.

Denise came in at first light of the morning, with breakfast. Belgium waffles, sage sausage, and freshly squeezed orange juice.

"I take it your date with Rob didn't go that well last night, huh?" Denise asked, after we'd finished eating.

"No it didn't," I gulped down my juice. "It was a disaster. I had to put him in his place. Girl, he was Mr. Gentleman in the beginning. So nice and mannerable, good conversation too, mostly about him. Come to think of it, he wasn't even trying to find out anything about me. But when we got to the club, he was all hands!"

"You're kidding!" Denise exclaimed. "What a loser!"

"Just one of many," I replied.

"Not all men are losers, Leslie. Don't give up. You'll find somebody," Denise said in an empathetic tone.

"That's the whole problem, I'm not trying to find anybody Denise! I've got things to accomplish, and to me, relationships only complicate shit, and keep you unfocused from what you really want to do. I should have just left that man where I found him. In how many different languages, and to how many people do I have to say this to, I am not trying to find anybody!" Denise only looked at me. She didn't know what to say. If I was her, I probably wouldn't know either.

in the house

"Hi Leslie, this is Elaine, your TIL building coordinator. How are you? I'm just calling to remind you that the reports are due tomorrow, you know what time. I know you won't disappoint me. Thanks."

"AAAyoo! Whatsup! This is Khalif, I'm in town, just thought I'd give you a buzz to see what you've been up to. Call me when you get in!"

"Damn! That's a long beep! Where are you girl? This is Rachelle. Well, anyway, call me at home later. Bye."

"Hello Leslie, this is your mother calling. I know you're away, but since you didn't leave a number where I could reach you at, I decided to call you. I just wanted to hear the sound of your voice, and let you know that I'm not dead yet. If you check these messages, call me as soon as you get it. I love you! Did I say that this was your mother?"

"Hello Leslie, this is the Super. I guess you're not home. Well, anyway, we need some oil; it's pretty low so if you could, please call the oil company. Thank you."

"Whaatsup yo? This is Jerkee speaking. I wish you would change that message on your machine, it sucks. I liked the other one better. Look, BFF is having a Production class on location managers, give me a call back if you want to go so that I can RSVP for both of us. Peace!"

"Hi Leslie! This is your little cousin Tracey calling! I just wanted to see how you were doing. I'm fine. I've started a new job for the summer. I'm taking care of young kids at a day camp. I'm not getting paid but they give me free lunch. It's pretty tasty too, if I must say so myself. How's your cat? Do you still have her, and is she still in heat? Where are you? Call me whenever you get the chance. Bye. . . ."

"Hey Leslie! Whazup! It's your cousin Rachelle again. Where the hell are you? I've got some serious things going on with me, and I really need to talk to you, like soon! Love you! Bye."

Let's see, shit I've got to do those reports, I can't turn them in late again. Khalif, I'd have to call him back, my mother, I love you too, mom. Hmph! Always something with this damn building! Couldn't they survive without me for two weeks? Jerkee, a.k.a. Mike, my friend, I'd have to call him back, anything production related was definitely a go. My little cousin Tracey, I often wonder, does she leave messages on the machine thinking it will actually answer back on its own? And what *did* ever happen to that cat? And my Cousin Rachelle, who I lovingly refer to as Cuz. She must have forgotten that I said I was going out of town. I'd have to talk to her later.

Aaaah. . . . All the comforts of home. It was good to be missed. My two-week vacation's already over, and now it's 7:30 in the morning, and here I am, listening to my phone messages, and calculating the figures on my tenant rent rolls to be submitted to TIL no later than nine a.m. this morning.

I carefully summed up the final numbers for the cash disbursement. Thank goodness they evened out. I'm such a last minute person. At least I can admit to that. Once I dropped those reports off, I could come back home, and relax. I could catch up on some things that really needed to be done, but never got done because I kept putting it off because of the big procrastinator I can sometimes be. Yes, that's what I'd do. I'd give my apartment a thorough cleaning. I'd straighten out my file cabinet. Maybe I'd even try to tackle cleaning out that refrigerator. What a life. My thoughts immediately went to my last conversation with Niece and the words, *"Don't worry, you'll find somebody."*

"Hmph, somebody like Mr. Slickster!" I said aloud to myself. After I took the reports downtown I came back uptown and you know who I bumped into. Yes, Mr. Slickster himself, and as usual, he was smiling. I think that's probably why I refuse to trust him, he smiles too damn much. There's just got to be something sneaky and wrong about that. He had seen me from across the street and was crossing over, apparently, to say something to me.

"Long time no see, stranger," he said.

"Yes I know. I had to get away for a little while, you know how it is," I said.

"Yeah, this city will drive you crazy if you let it. So where'd you go?" he asked.

"Philadelphia. A good friend of mine lives out there."

"Good ole Philly PA. huh? So did you find any brotherly love?"

"No, . . . I didn't. I can't honestly say that I was looking for any," I smirked.

"Well sometimes you don't have to look for it, it finds you," he said.

"Then I'm still waiting. Well, let me go," I told him, as I readjusted my bag over my shoulder.

"Where you going? You're always running off somewhere."

"People do that, you know," I answered.

"Okay if I drop by later? I mean, if you're not too busy or anything."

"I don't know about that, Mr. Slickster."

"Okay, now we're back on that again. Fine," he said, going his way, and me going mine. Somehow I knew we were going to meet again, and soon.

❖

"How you gonna win . . . when you ain't . . ." I sang out. I was cleaning and jammin, jammin and cleaning, full blast on my CD player *Lauryn Hill* style. Now all I had to do was get that damn refrigerator cleaned out, and I'd be done with everything. "You ain't right within . . ." BOOM!BOOM!BOOM! Was that somebody knocking on my door? "Just a minute!" I yelled out, turning the volume on my stereo down, and going to answer the door. I looked through the peephole, and again, it was Mr. Slickster, in the flesh. What in the hell was he doing here? Didn't I make it clear to him that I didn't want any company? And here he is, popping up right here at the foot of my door. Doesn't he know that I mean what I say? I thought, quickly smoothing over my clothes.

"Nice voice!" he said, after I'd opened the door.

I must have been a sight in those cut off shorts and that rainbow tie-dyed tank shirt. Grabbing a robe would've been nice. I was showing more skin than I'd wanted Mr. Slickster to see, but it was too late now. "You think?" I said, not sure if I was more embarrassed by the fact that he'd heard me sing, or caught me wearing next to nothing. "Naah, I can't sing, but thank you anyway." I'd answered. "Now what can I do for you?"

"Well, can I come in? I need to talk to you. It'll only be for a minute."

I sighed, "Alright, but just for a minute," I said letting him in and locking the door behind him. I wondered how he knew which apartment I lived in.

"Thank you. This is a pretty big place," he said, as he walked through the long hallway. "How many rooms is this?"

"Five and a half," I said.

"What's the half?"

"The bathroom. Have a seat," I told him.

"Thank you," he said again. "Are all of the apartments in the building set up like this?"

"Not really. You've seen apartment #19, that's

what most of them are like. I've been doing work on my own apartment," I told him.

"You know, I could fix this apartment up for you, make it like new. I'd start by taking off all of that old molding," he pointed out.

"Thanks, but no thanks." I was a bit offended by his offer. Had he been implying that I hadn't done a good job in fixing my own apartment? I was about ready to bring out the ammonia and mop, and wash his ass on out the door. "I'm perfectly happy with what I've done here," I said with attitude. "Besides, if I get my apartment completely fixed, everyone will want theirs fixed too," I added, disappearing into the bathroom to check my look. I snatched up a denim shirt that I'd hung over the shower rack and put it on.

"Well what's so wrong with that?" he asked. "We could work out a payment plan," he tells me.

"Is that what you came up here for? To offer me a payment plan?" I asked him angrily, neatly brushing my hair back into a ponytail. "I was right in the middle of doing something before you came by."

"No, it's not. You go to school right?" he asked me, quickly changing the subject.

"Yes," I answered as I came out of the bathroom. What had he come up here for?

"What are you taking up?"

"Video Production."

"Oh, I can see you there. Directing and calling

out shots. You seem to have a real knack for doing that," he said.

"I choose to take that as a compliment sir, and what about you?" I asked. "I know you work a lot. Do you own that building across the street?"

"Yeah, what I really want to do is get all of those tenants out, gut the whole building, and redo all the apartments in it. But those tenants aren't going anywhere, so instead, I'll just do one apartment at a time, and work on the major systems in the building. I already did the roof, and the sewer line is next," he said.

"How many units are there in the building?"

"Twelve when I'm done, right now there's eight. I plan on divvying it up."

"Oh, I see. More money, huh?" I replied. And it went on from there. We talked about everything from property to politics, and the words between us seemed to flow as if we had known each other for a lifetime. We were laughing and joking, and I even made us some sandwiches and iced tea. Then we listened to music and kept on talking, now it was about music. Turns out he's an opera freak, a Pavarotti and Kathleen Battle fiend. I must admit, it had been a nice evening. Before we knew it, it was one o'clock in the morning, and the only reason I knew the time was because the late, late movie had come on. *Lady Sings the Blues* was the feature film.

"It's one o'clock in the morning!" I said.

"No!" he said. "Already? Wow! I guess I'd better go, I don't want to wear out my welcome, and I've got a lot of work to do in the morning. What are you doing tomorrow?" he asked me.

"Let's see, tomorrow's Thursday, I've got classes and a few errands to run, that's about it. Why?"

"I don't know, I just thought maybe you'd like to go to the movies . . ."

"Fine," I said.

"Fine?"

"Fine! Now leave already before I change my mind," I joked, escorting him to the door.

"Goodnight, Leslie," he said.

"Goodnight, Benjamin." I know he was glad that I had called him by his given name, instead of "Mr. Slickster." I locked the door behind him. I couldn't believe that it had been so late. Where had the time gone? He was nice, very down to earth. A friendly kind of guy. A friend, that's all I wanted and nothing more. "Friend" being the operative word.

new friendships

Ready to roll tape and confirm speed."

"Speed!" the class yelled out in unison.

"In five, four, three . . ." the hush of the countdown could be heard by all over the microphone as it permeated via the speakers and out onto the main studio floor. My professor was preparing the class for our mid-term production projects by giving us a formatted demonstration of an on-air two-person guest and host talk show. His assistants operated the camera, switcher, VTR, and graphics while he stayed inside with the class directing from the control room. We were also getting the dates for our student production projects. No one else wanted to volunteer, so I decided to be the brave one and venture out where no one else dared to go; first. My date was set for two weeks from the day of class. I was thinking along the lines of doing my project based on a comedy format, a hair show, infomercial sort of thing. Yeah, I was definitely psyched about that. I knew just who I'd get to play the actors, a few friends from an acting class I had taken two semesters before. I'd call my infomercial "Hair Magic."

Professor Ortega decided to dismiss the class early on account of the demo so with all my errands run I could just head home and relax until later when my new-found friend and I would be going out. I guess it was safe to say that I was psyched about that too, although it was subconscious. I flicked on the television set, and instead of watching TV, the TV wound up watching me because I wandered off to sleep. I was awakened to the sound of a loud banging on my front door.

"I'm coming, I'm coming! Can't a person get a little rest in her own house?" I yelled, as I dragged my two feet behind me. I tripped over the checkered blue and white welcome mat that lay on the hallway floor. Right now, I hadn't felt like welcoming anyone, but I opened the door anyway. I hadn't even bothered to look through the peephole to see who it was.

"You know, you keep it up and I might start taking this abuse personally," Benjamin said as

he leaned against the wall alongside my ~~apart~~-
ment door.

"Abuse?" I asked him in a laugh-sleep state.

"Yes, abuse. Every time I come here I practically have to knock the door off the hinges before
I can get in!" he said.

"Oh, I'm sorry. It wasn't done on purpose. I fell
asleep. Oh my goodness! The movies, right?
Come in, come in, I completely forgot."

"You sure? I mean we can always do this some
other time. . . ." he offered.

"No, I'm sure it will only take a minute for me
to get myself together," I said, patting my hair,
thinking perhaps I'd have to add a zero on to that
minute. My hair would need a little work. "You
want something to drink or something?" I asked.

"No thanks, I'm okay."

"Well make yourself at home. The remote control is on the table if you want to change the station."

It seemed that he had already made himself
right at home, and was quite relaxed. When I
came out again, he had switched the TV to the
baseball game and had grabbed a coke from the
fridge. I made a superwoman change into my floral swing dress, platforms, and blue denim
jacket.

"Ready!" I said, pouncing out into the living
room. "Ten minutes, my fastest time ever!" I
could tell that he was pleased with my appear-

...ion on his face, and by the ...a hold of my hand even before ...the door.

...walked downstairs, and outside of the b...ng, I could feel the weight of something. *Something . . . was burning a big, black, crusty hole, eating its way through the back of my sundress.* It was the eyes of everyone on my street staring and whispering. About me, about Benjamin, and probably about the fact that we were walking together. Just wondering where or what we were going to do next so that it could fuel up their conversations for a trip that would last way into the night. And to tell the truth, it really bothered me. Benjamin must have picked up on my vibe, or maybe it was the way I kept turning around to look back as we walked.

"Don't pay those people any mind. They don't have anything better to do," he told me, pulling me onto the other side away from the curb. "No, you walk on the inside, a true gentleman always walks on the outside of a lady."

"So I see." A very correct gentleman at that. I guess I'd have to show those neighbors of mine that I did have something better to do, and I was going to do it. You know what's funny? When Benjamin first started working on my block, nobody noticed him. But just as soon as I started seeing him, every damn body knows him. Act like they go way back, but don't know him from Adam.

We went to see an alien action flick, one of those Will Smith movies. It was pretty good. Afterwards, we went to this Italian place to eat, Jagos, where we both enjoyed a romantic dinner. I ordered spaghetti and meatballs, and he ordered pasta primavera. After an appetizing meal, we headed back home to my apartment to cool out for the rest of the evening. Not to my surprise, the same people who were outside when we left were outside when we returned. Only this time around, nothing bothered me.

"These steps are a killer," Benjamin said as we climbed up the final landing leading to my door.

"Step training! That's what I call it!" I huffed.

"That's a good one!" he answered.

Once we were inside, I slipped in a CD, and took out the Scrabble board.

"How about a game of Scrabble?" I asked him.

"That's right up my alley, I love a challenge, but I had better warn you that I'm merciless when I'm in my competitive mode."

"Well I'm the Queen of Scrabble, and I say you're gonna lose, so bring it on!" I said as we began to play. "M-O-N-O-G-A-M-Y, that's a triple word score, one hundred and forty-one points."

"Monogamy?" he asked.

"Yes monogamy, haven't you ever heard of it before?" I said.

"Of course I have. I'm just trying to make sure that you're not cheating."

"Not with a word like monogamy I'm not." Well I didn't really claim the title Queen of Scrabble, but I wound up winning twice, and he won once.

"I told you that you'd lose!"

"Yeah you did, but somehow, I don't mind losing to you," he added. Our eyes locked into an intense stare that made me look away. It was like he was looking right through to my soul or some shit. "How old are you?" he asked me from out of the blue, as we tossed the tiny wooden square letters into their bag, packing the game away.

"Twenty-one, and you?"

"I'm an old man," he sighed. "I'm thirty-five."

He's thirty-five, and I'm twenty-one, that's . . . a fourteen-year age difference, *I counted to myself. Silence.*

"Is my age a problem to you?" I asked him.

"No, I don't see it as a problem at all. You're very mature for your age, I knew that when I first met you. I could tell, just by the way you carry yourself. I usually don't get involved with younger women. I think 29 is the youngest I've ever dealt with. You give me a hard time though," he said.

"Does that make me more mature? The fact that I'm not fawning all over you?"

"No."

"Then what? The challenge? The thrill in the chase? You just said yourself, you like a challenge."

"Yes, that's definitely a part of it, and you should feel flattered."

"Should I?" I laughed. "Oh thank you, Great man! You just say whatever I want to hear huh?"

"No, I say whatever I think. You asked me a question, and I gave you an answer."

The honesty thing, it was cute. I wondered how long it would last.

"Now here's a question for you. Is my age going to be a problem with you?"

I pondered the thought for a minute. "I don't think so . . . I don't know, I haven't really given it too much thought. You don't look that old."

"Gee—thanks."

I laughed, and hoped I hadn't hurt his feelings. "It's like you said," I told him, trying to clean things up, "I'm mature for my age, I can handle you."

"Mmmm," he murmured. "Now who's the one looking for a challenge?"

"Anyway, on a lighter note, hungry?"

"Leslie, we just ate!"

"That was hours ago, I'm still hungry," I said.

"You sure can eat!" he said. I went inside the safe haven of my kitchen and grabbed a bag of Doritos and a couple cans of soda.

"So, do you have any children?" I yelled out from the kitchen upon entering the living room.

"Yeah, I have a son," he answered.

I wasn't really surprised, most men did in this day and age.

"Really? How old is he?"

"Thirteen."

"Mmph, so where do you live?"

"Starrett City."

"Oh, you and your son?"

"Yeah, and his mother," he added in a nonchalant tone. There was a distinctive silence, the second one that night.

"You live with your son and his mother?"

"Yeah," he said again, as if I'd only asked him whether it was night or day outside.

Then I just had to ask, "Well are you together?"

"Together-together. . . . no, but we've lived together for the past six years."

"Okay, let me get this straight, you live with your woman, and your son. . . . and you're not together-together, but you've been together for the past six years? So what are you doing here?"

rachelle

Somewhere, in the far reaches of my mind, I knew I needed to get the hell away from Anthony. But how could something so wrong feel so right? How could it feel so right, and be so wrong? Until I met Anthony, I didn't know what an orgasm was. Looking back now on the 35 years of my life makes it feel like an eternity. *Mmph. Mmph. Mmph.* It's all that I can say when I think about all I've been missing out on. My husband screwed me for as long as my marriage lasted, that would be ten long years. But Anthony makes love to me, each and every time it's the way that I want it. He's sensitive to all my needs. . . . Just in the way he kisses me, not sloppy and quick, but slow, sensual, and deep . . . The way he makes those little circles directly beneath the circumference of my breast bone, and the way he strokes me . . . so, so, good.

Anthony definitely aims to please me . . . **Somehow I can't help but to love him . . .**

AND
THEN THERE'S

Eustace, my sexy dark Jamaican. Just thinking about those strong legs and muscular arms gets my pot to boiling. Eustace was a friend to me even before there ever was an Anthony. He's always there for me when I need an ear. If effort counts for anything, he definitely gets an A. A black stallion, **WHOOSH, WHOOSH, WHOOSH**, his thrusts are endless and hard. Feels like he's trying to break me in two sometimes. With Eustace, he aims to prove that he's the best, and that he can rock my world. But I've got news for him about that and a few other things. But still . . . **I LOVE HIM.**

Meet Rachelle, my cousin. A petite caramel complexioned thirty-five-year-old with a short close cut platinum blonde Caesar. Since she's in my family, I can honestly admit that she's got it going on. She's also got three children, though you could never tell by looking at her. There's two boys, Tyreek 4, and Jaree 6, and a girl, Zoie, who just turned 8. Rachelle's in the middle of a divorce from an over-obsessive husband who "resides behind bars," let's just say to put it mildly. All props go to Rachelle, holding down a full time office cleaning job from eight to four, running her own household, and taking care of herself and her three children. The only thing? My cousin, like so many others of us out there, is searching for that Mr. Right, and right now it just happens to be someone ten years her junior. You heard me, that man is named Anthony, and he's 21 with one kid and a little-above-minimum-wage job. He's pretty responsible, and seems to care a lot about Rachelle and her kids. He possesses those hard to find qualities that some women can't even find in a thirty-one-year-old.

And then there are other factors. . . . Like Eustace. Eustace is 29, attractive, and of Jamaican descent. If one were to compare his physical appearance, you would swear up and down that he and Supercat the reggae singer were brothers. He owns his own business, a small grocery store which lies smack dab in the center of Flatbush, Brooklyn. Oh, one more thing, Eustace's *Married*. He's practically a newlywed, just recently attached only four short months ago. Still, Rachelle manages to hold that special place in his life.

"Hello, Eustace?" Rachelle asked, after punching in the ten digits of her phone which would connect her directly to Eustace's line.

"Hey Sweetie, where are you?" Eustace asked, in his native Jamaican accent.

"Home, I'm off on Thursdays, remember?"

"Oh yeah right. The background is so quiet. Where are the kids?"

"Right about now, they had better be in day camp," Rachelle said, with a sense of relief. It was good to have a break from the Monday through Friday rigmaroles she had to endure with her own children. The 5:00 a.m. wake-up calls, making sure they were bathed, that teeth were brushed, and that all their hair was combed. Clothes got sorted, and shoes slipped on. Finally, there was the cereal scenario. Always a fight over who would get to hold the box. She was glad that they were where they were. She loved her kids, but she needed to have some time for herself once in a while. Especially on a day off.

"So you have some free time on your hands . . . Why don't you come down and see me?" Eustace asked.

"Now? All the way out to Brooklyn? For what, Eustace?"

"I miss you, I'm thinking maybe you and I could . . . get together."

"Is that all you ever think about, getting together?"

"When it comes to you, it's hard to think about much of anything else."

"You don't say. I hardly believe that you think of me when you go home to your wife every night," Rachelle blurted out, knowing damn well that he didn't. Did he think he could just say anything he wanted to her and be able to get away with it? He certainly had not thought of her enough to not marry the wife. Then again, who said she was ready to be married again? Better that woman than her. She was nowhere ready to try marriage a second time around so soon.

"Hold on, Rachelle. Make sure you check that delivery against my list before you unload those boxes!" he told some men in his store. "Yeah," Eustace said, resuming his conversation on the phone with Rachelle in a loud tone. "So you coming over or not?" he asked again.

"Well that might be kind of hard, because my car's broken. The mechanic says I need a new transmission."

"How much is it?" Eustace asked.

"$700."

"I wish I could help, Sweetie," Eustace answered abruptly, "but right now business is kind of slow. I really don't have it."

Rachelle took in a deep breath of air.

"So what was the point in asking me how much it would cost to fix it?" Just then she remembered her last one-on-one talk with Eustace. She had made it very clear that under no uncertain terms would she tolerate the treatment she was getting from him. Sure, he was there when she needed someone to talk to. But somehow, that just wasn't enough anymore. There was going to have to be a change. After all, she was his mistress, and in Rachelle's mind, mistresses shouldn't have to want for anything. He was looking out for his wife and kids, well what about her needs? She had bills in excess, and all on a single household income to run. Always claiming to be her man and all of that. He'd said that he understood and that he'd handle things, sure he would.

"Look Eustace, my lousy car finally breaks down, and you mean to tell me that you can't give me any money towards getting it fixed? And you're calling yourself my man?"

"Rachelle, I am your man and I want to help you, but believe me baby, I just don't have it right now. Maybe in a couple of weeks, when business picks up."

"Check this out Eustace, a couple of weeks will be too little, too late. I got more than enough responsibilities over here. You're not there for me. How are my kids supposed to get back and forth to school? I need my car, Eustace, I'm not saying that I expect the world from you, but some help once in a while can't hurt. I really shouldn't have to ask you anyway. You should just be looking out for me like that," Rachelle continued in an angry tone, "the way I look out for you."

"Next week."

"Next week what, Eustace?" Rachelle asked, closing her eyes and taking a moment to breathe. It was all she could do to stay calm.

"I'll give you a little something."

"What's a little something? Something very close to $700, I hope."

"I'll see."

"You know what? No, just forget it, Eustace. Look, I gotta go."

"So you coming over or what?"

"Or what," Rachelle answered in a sarcastic tone. She couldn't believe he was still harping on her coming over.

"What does that mean?"

"It means good-bye Eustace, just good-bye." Click was the only sound to be heard as Rachelle hung up the phone. *The nerve*. "He's got the nerve to have an attitude with me!" Rachelle yelled, hurling salt and pepper shakers across the room. "What I need to do is get out of this mess I call a relationship." She bent over and rested her head onto the table, using her arms as pillow rests. Her head, clouded with disappointment, suddenly felt as though it was carrying the weight of her whole body. Almost as if dazed, she thought about the physical attraction Eustace held over her. She had also admired the fact that he was in control of his own business. But what did any of that have to do with her? Those were just excuses. Lately, she had found herself doing a lot of that. From her he got sex and companionship. If only Anthony could have helped. Him and his old good lovin' broke ass. Well screw Eustace. There were other things she could occupy her time with. Rachelle took a look around her spacious two-bedroom apartment only to see disarray everywhere by the children she was proud to call her own. The tiny five-finger handprints and smudges from the walls and refrigerator, the piles of colored red, orange, and yellow socks and pants scattered throughout. Not to mention the toys from underneath the bed and on top of the dressers which barely left a clear spot in the room. Those kids have more clothes than they'll ever need to wear in a child's lifetime, Rachelle thought to herself starting to tidy up. When she was done, the place was immaculate. She opened the refrigerator to get something to drink, but only one swallow of orange juice remained in the half-gallon container. Rachelle gulped down the last bit, straight from the carton, doing something she told the kids never to do. She got some cash together, and went food shopping. Finally, there were the three large loads of laundry she had to do. The door buzzer rang in the midst of the third load. Anthony had come in with the kids.

"Mommie!"

"Mommie!"

"Hi Mommie!" the kids yelled out.

"Hey sweethearts!" Rachelle said, giving each one of her children a tight embrace, and a kiss on the cheek.

"Mommie, I'm hungry!" Jaree said.

"Mommie, Jaree scratched me!" Tyreek yelled.

"So, you kicked me!" an even louder Jaree screamed out in retaliation.

"Mommie, can we go to the park?" Zoie asked.

"No, we just came from the park," Anthony said.

"I know, but I want to go back again! I didn't have a chance to get on the super slide!"

"No, I think you guys have had enough excitement for one day," Rachelle told them. "Go run your baths, you kids are filthy and tired."

"I'll do it," Anthony volunteered, no sooner said than done complete with bubbles and bath toys for the boys, and the Secret Garden video cassette set up and playing in the room for Zoie. "Now where's my hug and kiss?" he asked, as he came up from behind Rachelle.

"Right here," Rachelle said, as she turned around to give Anthony a deep long kiss.

Anthony lifted her up onto the gray Formica kitchen counter top, leaving her legs open to dangle over its edge. Anthony kissed her back something lovely.

"Mmph . . . we'd . . . better . . . stop . . ." Rachelle said in between kisses.

"Why?" Anthony asked.

"Because the kids . . . I promise . . . as soon as . . . they go to bed . . . Anthony, you know how you get me . . ." That couldn't have been more true. Rachelle was dripping like a leaky sink faucet.

"Alright, I'll let you go for now, but I'm going to do you right later, that's a promise," he said, giving her one tight squeeze and peck on the forehead. "What's for dinner, Boo?"

"What would you like?"

"You," Anthony said as he kissed Rachelle up and around her neck.

"Anthony stop!" Rachelle said playfully. "I know, how about roast chicken, scalloped potatoes, a nice tossed salad, and a chocolate cake for dessert?" Rachelle asked.

"Bring it on!"

"Okay, then that's exactly what I'll order from the take-out menu from BBQ's!" Rachelle answered, making Anthony laugh.

"I know that you didn't seriously think that I was going to cook all that food at this hour. It wouldn't be done until midnight!"

"Mommie, Jaree's getting water in my eyes!"

"Stop it!" the two boys screamed from the bathroom, splashing water all over the floor.

"Well I guess it's time to get those kids out," Rachelle said. "Let me go and put Zoie in next."

After the food arrived, the kids ate, and were put to bed. Rachelle plugged in the nite light, and tucked the kids in.

"Movie?" Anthony asked as Rachelle closed the door to the children's bedroom.

"I'd rather watch you," Rachelle answered with a smile.

"Oh yeah?" Anthony lifted his shirt off over the top of his head, and then Rachelle's, kissing her everywhere. It was all the encouragement he needed. He went down, down, down, making no stops. Anthony was going downtown on the tongue express.

"Choo-choo! choo-choo!" Rachelle screamed out. "Choo-choo!" She screamed out again. It was just the beginning. Anthony had suggested that they try something new. It involved a single chair, turned on its side.

"That was the best, Boo," Anthony said.

"Yes it was," Rachelle replied. She was rendered almost speechless. It was real good to her. It always was.

"Boo?" Anthony asked.

"Yes?"

"I wanna help you get your car fixed. I'll work overtime if I have to. At another building maybe. Something."

"Alright Anthony, but you don't have to."

"No, I want to . . . I'm saying Boo, I'm your man, I'm supposed to do it. You shouldn't even have to ask!" Rachelle rolled over and turned on her back to stare at the top of the smoothed bedroom ceiling.

"Alright Anthony," Rachelle answered calmly. It was sounding all too familiar, but not familiar enough. Anthony drifted off to sleep, his snores posing the evident sign of satisfaction. But Rachelle lay awake still staring at that damn ceiling.

no strings

Not that I want to do it, but I have to. See, I met this guy at a supper club on the Upper West Side one night, Sean's his name. His attraction to me then was instant, and has been ongoing for the past three months now. I'd say that I had it going on when we met. My dress was cute, not too short or too tight cause I respect myself, I'm a woman. Though with my shape it doesn't take much for me to fill out a dress. It's a bright lime-green number with spaghetti straps. It's good to know that after three kids, I still got it. As I can remember, all of the men in the club wanted me.

"Can I buy you a drink?"

"What about a dance?"

It's what they asked. But my Mr. Man won me

right over. He never asked, he just did, gliding over to my table with that shiny fine bottle of Cristal Champagne for me and all my girlfriends. He didn't wait for my stomach to start growling either, taking me and my two girlfriends who were with me, out for lobster dinners. To top it all off, he drove all my friends home, then me, and I didn't even have to give him any. Not a kiss. What I did give him was my telephone number, and he's been calling me ever since. All we do is talk on the phone.

I told him I had a man, but he says that true love should be able to withstand a little competition. He's got a point there. But then again, he also says that he's going to marry me. To that I say, *Sure*. Just let him keep hope alive with that one. I was talking to him the other night and happened to mention the situation with my car, and he agreed to give me the money. No strings. Let's see, I believe his exact words were,

"I'm giving you the money because I like the person you are."

Please. At first I wasn't going to take it, but forget that, I need my car, and I don't see Eustace giving me the money and Anthony just doesn't have it. So I've gotta do what I gotta do. Period.

It really wasn't that bad, and I got the money. No, it's not what you think, I did not sleep with Sean.

He took me out to eat and then we went back to his apartment. It's real nice. Zebra-skin rugs, all black and white furniture, and a spiral staircase that leads to the upstairs of his duplex. He fixed us some mixed drinks, then slipped into a black satin robe with nothing underneath, buck naked. I knew he was from the minute he sat down, because his stuff was all over the place after the belt on his bathrobe "just happened" to come loose. But all he wanted me to do was touch his body, to make him hard. All my clothes stayed on the entire time. He did kiss me though, I really didn't mind that. The worst though, was that I did let him put these two huge hickeys on my neck. It happened so fast. And now I'm sure that it happened on purpose. I think Sean really got off on the fact that I was spending time with him, and not the man I told him I'm so in love with. I know damn well that I'm too old for the hickey nonsense, but what's done is done. And that's exactly what I'm about to be if Anthony sees this shit. Done. The ice just wasn't working. I dug my compact from out of my bag, and covered the two huge red blotches with some of Zani's Shades of Natural foundation as best I could. A turtleneck would be perfect right about now, but not with it being 85 degrees outside. That just wasn't happening, and I had to get my kids. I can't very well leave them at the damn Center all day and night.

Why in the hell did that boy have to work right downstairs? He liked to shock the hell out of me when I first saw him, in that little burgundy uniform and matching monkey hat. Standing up all straight and upright in the front of my lobby. But he's working, it's a job, and he does have his whole life ahead of him after all. Well, here goes nothing, Rachelle thought to herself. Just as she was about to head out of the apartment, there was a sudden knock at the door. Rachelle panicked as she looked through the peephole. Oh God it was Anthony! There was little·else she could do. Rachelle slowly turned the knob and cracked open the door.

"Hey Boo! Listen, my mom's gonna pick up the kids today. C'mon open up the door, what's wrong with you?" Anthony asked her.

Rachelle opened the door a little wider, and Anthony went on to push the door fully open.

"Nothing, nothing's wrong," Rachelle stood away from the door and said, "Your mom's gonna pick the kids up? Oh-okay, I was just on my way down to get them," Rachelle stammered, sensing she was setting herself up to be busted.

"That's what I just said you silly rabbit, now where's my hug?" Anthony asked, taking a hug, just happening to look down to see brown splotches covering the once red hickeys. "Yo, what's that shit on your neck?"

"Nothing," Rachelle answered. That nothing response was bound to come back and haunt her.

"Nothing?" Anthony grabbed Rachelle's chin and pushed it upward so that her neck stood long and exposed under the bright fluorescent kitchen lights. "That's a fuckin hickey!" Anthony said, after wiping one of the make-up blotches off on his hand. "It's two!"

Rachelle didn't know Anthony's voice could go down that deep.

"I don't believe you!" Anthony hollered out, with red, bleary eyes.

"Wha-at?" Rachelle asked dumbfoundedly.

"What the fuck that's what! You're actually standing in my face trying to lie to me!"

"Anthony no I'm not! You don't understand. If you let me explain . . ."

"Yo, I can't even trust you. . . . I would have expected this from one of those little young chickenheads, but you? A grown woman? I understand alright! I'm out!"

"Anthony!" Rachelle called out—but by then it was already too late, he was gone.

❖

Hell. Hell could best describe the way the past few weeks had been going. Who says you need a man in your life to be happy? Rachelle thought to herself, as she pushed down the button on her tape player to hear Toni Braxton's cassette of *Just Another Sad Love Song*. She had played that same song at least a dozen times. Over and over and over, singing each word with all the feeling and furor Toni must have felt as she sang it. Rachelle's version was louder and way off key, but comparably, the lyrics in the song mirrored her life. Her life had been diminished to just another sad love song. On top of that, her answering machine remained in constant motion screening each and every call, none being important enough to spark an interest in Rachelle's attention span. The phone seemed to ring every hour on the hour.

Ring, ring. Shit, there it goes again, Rachelle thought to herself. Couldn't a girl just be left alone to sulk by herself once in a while?

"Hello, you've reached. . . . Sorry we can't come to the phone. . . ." her machine chimed in.

"Hello Rachelle, it's your mother, I'm calling long distance, so pick up. I know you're there."

Rachelle hated the fact that her mother knew she was home. "Yeah Ma, I'm here," Rachelle said reluctantly, picking up the telephone receiver.

"Were you asleep?" her mother asked.

"Yeah, I was knocked out," Rachelle said, turning the music down, throwing in a fraudulent yawn. The last thing she needed was for her mother to suspect that something was wrong. Especially when it really was. Even if she did tell her the truth, she'd find a way to convince her that it was something else. Perhaps some missing link or deep-rooted psychological problem. Her mother would probably suggest counseling.

"How are the kids?" Rachelle asked.

"They're all fine. They went with your uncle James on a nature hike. They've been gone since morning. I know they'll be knock-down tired when they get back. They're loving it down here. It's such a good environment for them. I sprayed some OFF bug repellent on the kids so that they wouldn't come back with a bunch of mosquito bites," her mother said.

"That's good Ma," Rachelle replied in an unconvincing tone. She wished she could spray on a little mother repellent on herself every once in a while. "Well, tell the kids that I love them, and that I'll see them when they get back home on Wednesday," Rachelle said, trying to bring the conversation to a rapid close.

"Are you okay?" Rachelle's mother asked. "You don't sound so good. You really should be getting out, now that the kids aren't there," she added.

"I know, I know. I will, and yes, I'm fine, just a little tired that's all. Anyway, let me let you go Ma."

"Okay, take care."

"You too," Rachelle replied.

Rachelle was glad the kids weren't there to see her in this mood, and the jumbled state she'd left the apartment in. She was always after them about picking up after themselves. It was good that the car was running, but she didn't feel like going anywhere, which only meant that it wasn't worth it. Mr. Man Sean would just have to find another fan because she wasn't the one. That fast life, and flashy business, didn't seem to have a place in her life at the moment, nothing did. There just was no get up and go. The only go Rachelle did have left was the go that sent her off to work each morning, and straight back home each evening. She only stopped off to get groceries or an occasional magazine at the local news stand. Her life, in summarization. And like a drop of rain it suddenly hit her. All of this seclusion wasn't making her feel any better. What was she going to do? Mope around for the rest of her life? It was high time she came out and faced reality. Rachelle decided she was going to do something about it. She got up, and changed the music tape, Step One. Step Two, she got dressed. She put on something real cute, a two piece-skirt suit with a bright orange cropped jacket. Step Three, she was out of the house and on her way to her best friend and cousin Leslie's house, who she also lovingly referred to as "Cuz." It had been too long since she had seen her, and they had a lot of catching up to do.

something in common

Beep! Beep! Beep! Beep! The car honked, drowning out the sounds of my television, whose usual volume setting was always closest to high or the virtually-deaf mode.

"Who's making all of that noise outside?" I said, as I sprung up from the couch over to the bedroom window to see who it was.

"Hey Cuz!" Rachelle yelled out from down below out of her small white Toyota car window.

"Hey Cuz!" I yelled back, sticking my arm out after her.

"What are you doing? Come down!"

"Alright!" I yelled back loudly. And why not? I hadn't seen my cousin since before I left for Philly. Lately, I'd been so preoccupied that I hadn't gotten a chance to get over and see her and the kids. I didn't know how I was going to tell her about Benjamin. Don't get me wrong, Rachelle and I could talk about anything, but I wasn't so sure about how she would handle this one, the news of my involvement with an almost married man. I went downstairs and got into the front seat of the car, slamming the door behind me.

"Where are the kids?" I asked Rachelle.

"With my Mom in North Carolina. Cuz, I want to get this out of the way now," Rachelle said as we sped down the street. "I gotta story. Like to hearit? Wellhereit goes," Rachelle mocked.

"What? Is something wrong?" I asked, pulling my seat belt over myself clicking it into place.

"No, I have good news, and I have bad news."

"Give me the good news first," I told her.

"Well the good news is that I've found somebody new. It's not gonna be all about Eustace no more. This guy is really good to me and the kids. Last week he made dinner for everybody. Spaghetti, garlic bread, the whole nine Cuz, and he washes dishes too!"

"Go-on girl! So what's the bad news?"

"The bad news is that. . . ."

"C'mon Cuz, spill it!"

"The bad news is that he's twenty-one."

"He's twenty-one?"

"Yeah, go ahead say it! Tell me how I'm crazy, and how I can get better. . . ."

"Well to tell you the truth Cuz, I'm not going to

say that. I really don't know that age matters all that much. Look at me. I'm 21, he's 35."

"Are you serious?"

"Very much so," I answered. All of a sudden Rachelle and I started screaming out at the top of our lungs.

"Tell me everything," Cuz yells. So I tell her everything there is to know about Benjamin and me.

"So, what do you think?" I asked Rachelle.

"I think that you need an older man, you're more mature than most your age."

"But Cuz, didn't you hear me? I said that he lives with another woman. Isn't that settling?"

"In a way, but for now why don't you just settle for a friendship? He's not married, and if he really was happy in his relationship with who-ever he lives with, then believe me he wouldn't be with you." Beep!Beep! Rachelle honked at a woman who was outside of the crosswalk. Beep! Beep! Rachelle honked again. "Move out of the way lady! Damn people act like they own the street or something!" Rachelle yelled out. "All I'm sayin is, that it's early. Take time and see where his head is at, that's all. I mean it can't hurt to try."

"True, very true," I agreed. Then she tells me everything about her and her guy. How she met Anthony bringing in bags from the supermarket. How he helped her upstairs, and how she asked him while he was there, if he knew how to hook up a cable box, and the rest was history.

"Oh yeah Cuz, there's just one more thing I forgot to tell you about Anthony and me. I messed up big time. I went to see my friend Sean and he looked out for me with my car and everything. We wouldn't be driving now if he hadn't. He also gave me these gigantic hickies. See?" It was faded, but I could still see where the marks were. They looked kind of purplish now.

"Anthony saw it and flipped. Cuz, he left me. So now it's like, I don't know what to do. I really like him Cuz. I think he's just what I need in my life."

"Damn Rachelle, you messed up. Why'd you do that?" I asked.

"Because, Anthony is great okay, he's all a woman could ask for, except for the fact that he works downstairs in my lobby making a little above minimum wage! Realistically speaking, that can't cut it Leslie, and you know it!"

"So it's over between you two? You and Anthony, I mean."

"Hell no! I'm getting him back." Rachelle pounded a fist onto the steering wheel and added, "I've got to."

"Well you can start making the guy feel like you know Cuz, or you are definitely gonna lose him."

"Yeah, I know right, and I definitely do not want to lose him. Any suggestions?"

"Okay, my turn. What I would suggest is . . . You know that advice you just gave me? Well I thought it was real good. So good that I think that you should take a few lessons from yourself."

Rachelle narrowed her eyes and twisted her lips together as if to say: *Now why didn't I think of that?* "You know you're right," Rachelle said. "People are always quick to give advice that they wouldn't follow themselves. Following my own advice might just be an avenue worth exploring."

"That's the best thing I've heard you say today," I told her.

"So where do you want to go now?" Rachelle asked me.

"City Island?"

"Right again!" we both exclaimed loudly laughing and heading for the expressway.

new awakenings

You know what? Fine. He has his family, and I, being the humanitarian that I am, couldn't be happier for him. According to Rachelle, it's alright to just be friends. But it's what I think that's important. After all, it is my life. Friends? I mean, that's all we are anyway but I guess what I hate to admit most is the truth. I was really starting to like him. Why'd he have to go and make me start doing that? Well, better I find out now than later. At least he was honest with me. He could have lied. *I live alone.* It's not that difficult to say. *I live alone.* Who knows how far it would have gotten him. Not very, knowing me. Either way he loses out. I hardly consider myself the type to go getting involved with someone who's already involved with someone else. Getting all caught up, falling in love. Nope. Besides, everybody knows that the man never leaves his family for the other woman.

Life goes on. I'm getting ready to meet my friend Monica and her two friends downstairs. They're coming to pick me up to go to the movies. So I'm out, out of my mind. I get downstairs and he's standing right there, on the front landing of my stoop. I'm beginning to think that he has electronic radar or something.

"Hey," he said.

"Hello," I said in my keepin-it-simple tone.

"Going out?" he asks.

"Yes, I am."

"Can I go?"

"No," I said with a delay. "I don't think so."

"Why not?"

"Because it's ladies night. No men are allowed."

"I see. You sure now?"

"Positive," I answered in my sternest voice. I looked up the block to see if Monica was coming. I wish she'd hurry up. Alas, no cars passed through. I might as well have been in the Sahara desert somewhere.

"I like those shoes," Benjamin said as he looked down at my feet.

"Thank you." What? He liked my shoes? When was he going to give up? I thought to myself. I fiddled with the bottom button on my shirt. He was starting to make me fidgety.

"You lose my telephone number?"

"No."

"Then why don't you ever call me?" he persisted.

"Benjamin, you know exactly what the situation is, so let's not play out this little scenario of yours." Finally, some cars were coming through the block. Neither one of the two had Monica in it.

"So how's the building coming along?" he asked, as he smoothly changed the subject. He was good at that.

"Fine."

"Okay, I give up. I get the message. You don't feel like being bothered. So have a good time, maybe I'll see you later then." He walked across the street and got into his car, and drove off without looking back.

"Come on Leslie! Let's go!" Monica yelled. Suddenly the car that I had been searching so desperately for five minutes ago had appeared from nowhere. And I can't figure out for the life of me why I was wishing I was getting inside Benjamin's car instead of the one I was in.

❖

I hadn't seen him in twenty-one days, and I couldn't seem to get him out of my head, wasn't like I didn't try either. I did everything to keep my mind off him. Movies, parties, dinner, school, the building. I started out destination free, and now here I am, with my size nine feet leading me in close proximation of his building. I'm just hoping he's in there working. All I want to do is say hello, and to maybe see how he's doing. Leslie Williams, just that kind of lady. Yes. I recognized the man I saw. It's wasn't Benjamin, but he often worked alongside him.

"Is Benjamin here?" I asked.

"No, he's in the brownstone around the corner, Building 55. Go ahead, he's there," the man urged on.

With no further encouragement needed, I kindly thanked him, and headed around that corner to the brownstone. I looked up at the window. He was in there alright, I could see him standing atop a scaffold knocking down the ceiling.

"Benjamin!" I called up at him. He looked down and extended a friendly wave out to me.

"Be right there, hon." He was down in no time. "This is a surprise," he said, knocking the specks of flying white plaster from his hair and clothing as came from out of the building. "Miss me?" he asked.

"Should I have?" I chuckled.

"I love your style," he said, as he looked me over from head to toe. Subconsciously, it was no accident that I'd dressed myself in a cute cool bright tangerine skirt and tank ensemble.

"Long time no see for you too, huh?" I told him.

"Yeah I know. I've been working on my house in Queens putting in some new plumbing. Anyway," he said taking a seat on the ledge of the brownstone steps, "I didn't think you cared whether or not you ever saw me again. You kind of made that real clear three weeks ago."

"You've been counting the days?" I asked coyly.

"Twenty-one. Does that constitute grounds for us to go out Leslie?"

Going out . . . I thought as I watched the street lights change from a bright red stop to a flashy green go. Two friends . . . knowing myself and my limits, and knowing the kind of inner strength that I possess, was all that allowed me to cave in and give a willing nod of the head.

"Let's say tomorrow, around eleven. I just have a few stops to make, and then we can go from there."

"Are you going to tell me where it is that we're going? I mean, you're not planning on abducting me are you?"

"No. Wherever I take you I want it to be something you want to do. Don't worry, you'll like where we're going."

"I'd better," I said, as I walked away.

"Leslie."

"Yes?" I turned.

"Thanks for stopping by."

"You're welcome," I smiled. "But you don't have to thank me. I'm just that kind of lady."

"No, you mean, you're just my kind of lady."

Pardon? I was his kind of lady? Boy, was he in for a surprise.

✦

"I'm not going. I have nothing to wear!" I insisted, throwing myself down onto my bed. My best outfits were already laid out, completely covering the parameters of my full size bed, twice layered. After three try-on's I'd decided to go with the peach halter top outfit and silver sling-back sandals. "Cutesy, real cutesy," I said, giving myself one last superstar twirl in the bedroom mirror before heading downstairs to meet Benjamin. He wasn't there. Not a problem that he wasn't the most punctual person in the world. Who was? I'd just wait a few minutes. At eleven-fifteen his car pulled up. He was dressed in a light blue denim shirt and some blue jeans.

"You're late," I said as I walked over to the car. "What's all of this?"

"The reason why I'm late. I had to stop by the warehouse to get some more plywood. Seems I didn't have as much as I thought I did and this was the only time that I'd be able to get it." There were about ten sheets strapped around the roof of his car.

"Now where are we going?" I asked after hopping inside the car.

"It's a surprise." It was business before pleasure I guess because we did go drop the plywood off uptown. Then we drove towards the east side to look at some residential property Benjamin was thinking about buying.

"Next stop, the Marina," Benjamin said.

"Nice surprise," I looked over and told him. I don't think we could have picked a better day. The sky never looked so blue. What I wanted to know was this: What ever happened to that young woman who only wanted to be friends?

Once we got to the Marina, we held hands and took a stroll over to the other side along the Pier. We took in the fresh smell of the salt water and the sounds which made up the calming rush of the waves as they rocked back and forth against the rocks. There was no other place I would have rather been.

"I wish that life could always be this simple," Benjamin said to me.

"Life is simple. It's the people who live in it that make it so complex. I believe that people are in control of their own destinies. You can make things happen for yourself."

"Really?"

"Yes, really," I answered, with my Mayan-Civilization aged self. It was just then that Benjamin reached over to give me a big hug. Don't ask me what that was all about, because I'm not even sure, but I reciprocated with open arms. Then we took a stroll back over to the other side and got a couple of hot-dogs and sodas to tide us over until later. We sat at the shore and ate. We hugged some more, and we kissed. Our first kiss. Our kisses were like butter. We could do it all day. It was all very innocent, like big brightened eyes of a toddler baby. *Boy could he kiss*.

Everyone who saw us that day at the Marina seemed to pick up on our positive vibes, and indeed, life couldn't be sweeter. That is, until Benjamin's beeper went off.

"One of those guys is beeping me. Let me go see what's going on. Now if I can just find a pay phone."

"I think I saw some over where we parked the car," I told him.

"You did? That's my girl. I'll be right back," Benjamin said, giving me a quick peck on the lips, and getting up to go to the phone. Watching him walk his walk was better than taking in any sights the Marina had to offer. As I sat there alone looking out over the distance of the water, I reflected, reminding myself that *I* was the one in control of my destiny, and that *I* could make this relationship work. Why couldn't it? Surely, there were people in this world who were only staying in their relationships for the sake of convenience, be it the kids, the house, the money. What a way to live, I thought. A sympathetic side of mine was starting to go into overtime.

"Hon, you ready?" Benjamin came up to me and asked.

"Why? Do you have to go back to work?"

"No, there's no rush if you want to stick around a little longer."

"Not really, I guess we can leave," I answered. Benjamin extended his hand out to me, intertwining his fingers into mine to help me up. He continued to hold on tightly, as we walked back to the car. Afraid to let me go maybe? Just maybe.

We laid across the bed munching on some southern fried chicken I'd made after we came from the Marina. Benjamin started to laugh.

"What's so funny?" I asked.

"You've got food on your face."

"I've got food on my face?" I repeated.

"You've got a little chicken crumb right there on the side of your cheek."

"And I didn't get enough napkins," I said.

"Let me get it," he offered. Benjamin edged in closer to me, leaning over to lick the chicken crumbs off my face. His lips wandered closer onto mine, with a tongue that gently probed and parted, finding its rightful place in the hot center of my mouth. "Mmph, you're some kind of kisser . . . I love your mouth, it's so wet," he said.

"You're not so bad yourself," I said, as I lingered on the edge of his chin.

And that's how it started. However, I didn't let it start that much. I'm still a virgin. He'd just have to wait until I was ready. From there, we became almost inseparable, except when he was working, which he did a lot of. Whether he was knocking down walls or building them up, he always made time for me. I found myself doing things that I wouldn't ordinarily do like preparing special lunches, trying new dinner recipes, and taking longer to get myself to look just right. I was going all out with no time to spare for anyone besides Benjamin and myself. Not even Patrice, who by the way, I hadn't heard from since before I'd first met Benjamin. She must have been doing her own thing. Anyway, I was used to not hearing from her when she was involved. Right about now, I could relate. Denise was right, finding somebody finally did happen. I just couldn't resist writing several letters letting her in on the good news. I told her all about Benjamin, and my new found experiences in pre-sexually active-hood, detail by detail. The only thing that I didn't tell her was that he lived with another woman. I just couldn't bring myself to telling her that part. She was just so excited that I was in love and all. I wasn't going to be the one to ruin it for her. And as for Ms. Patrice? I could call her later. She's one I definitely want to wait to call, because she knows everything before I can even tell her.

There was only one person who could truly identify with me, and that was Rachelle. Who would have ever believed that we would both be in the same situation, both unplanned and totally unexpected. I really don't think that she knows what she has yet, but I'd give her some time. I know what I have. I'm feeling pretty close to Benjamin now, but at the same time it still feels wrong. Is that possible?

the other woman

I heaved a sigh of relief after writing out some tenant rent receipts and balancing the Tenants Association checkbook for the month. I hated accounting, be it any form, shape, or fashion. It was so tedious. A guaranteed minimum of two hours work. Thank goodness the worst was over. Especially on a beautiful day like this, I thought to myself. Not too hot or too cold, 80 degrees and hardly any humidity in the air. No need for the clitter-clang motion of my tired old metal fan, or the silence of my overpriced state-of-the-art Con Edison bill-loving air conditioner.

My stomach made a tiny grumble, reminding me that I hadn't eaten for the day. Maybe I'd make some lunch for Benjamin and myself. Tuna salad sounded good. "Mmph," I mumbled, I better make sure he's downstairs before I make anything. Going over to the window, I peer down at the building below. His car's out there, good. But something tells me not to go back in, not just yet. I glance over to see Benjamin coming from out of the building he's working on. I'm hoping he's not leaving. I'd call out to him, but that's not really my style, yelling out no damn window, I mean. Then, from out of nowhere it seems, this woman gets out of his car. Yes, his car. I'd seen the vehicle, but not her in it. *Right*. So she gets out, brown skinned, fairly attractive, if you like that curvaceous, bouncy haired type of woman. My instincts, which are in rare form, convince me that it has to be her. I am not believing this. Benjamin took his time going over to her. There was no kiss nor any kind of embrace. Apparently, he was just showing her the building and I guess the work that they had done thus far. I was heated, but did I really have a right to be? I mean, he told me what the situation was from jump street. But why did she have to come on the block, where I lived? *"Cause that's where her man's at, Stupid,"* I said aloud to myself. Stupid wasn't exactly the word I had in mind for myself.

My eyes only saw the interior of my four walls that day, and I made sure I cut that telephone ringer off. I never made that tuna salad either, which is probably to blame for this headache from hell. I started to call Rachelle, but I decided against it. Despite the circumstances, the day seemed to go by quickly. It was just how I wanted it to go. My front doorbell rang. I'm not going to answer it, I don't feel like being bothered, I thought. The knocking started again. Whoever it was certainly was persistent. I bet I knew just who it was. I finally went to the door to take a look through the peephole to have my suspicions confirmed. I opened the door.

"Hey, were you sleeping?" Benjamin asked, taking me into his arms and giving me a big hug and a kiss.

I stood there stiffly. "What's wrong?"

"Like you don't know," I said, locking the door. I released myself from his arms and walked into the living room. "Benjamin, I don't know if this is going to work!" I said, working up as much anger as I could. Believe me, it wasn't all that hard.

"Let's go for a drive, I have to go and pick up some money from some tenants in Queens."

"Fine," I told him. A ride would give me a chance to say what I had to say, and he'd have no choice but to give me feedback.

We drove to Queens with very few words said between us. I sat in the car and flashed back to Benjamin and the woman and their little meeting earlier. The millions of planned questions I'd intended on asking were steadily dwindling, down to none. *Think, Leslie, think,* I told myself. I just needed a few minutes to get what I wanted to say together. Okay, I was ready. "Benjamin, this is not going to work."

"You said that already."

"No, I mean it. I'm not the kind to settle . . ."

"Wait, don't tell me. You saw her, right?"

"How could I not have? How could you tell her to come and see you here? You know that this is where I live and that there was a chance I could run into her!"

"What was I supposed to do, ban her from the block? Look hon, I can't tell you what to do, and you know what the situation is. You need to know that I would never intentionally hurt you, but I can't make you any guarantees. There's always going to be a risk when you're involved in this kind of relationship," he said, looking over at me and then back to the road. "You'll have to decide . . ."

My eyes were swelled up with water, but I managed to hold the tears back. If felt like the end. We went on to collect the rents. Benjamin owned two houses in Queens that he rented out, residential properties.

"These people drive me crazy, it's always some song and dance with them when it's time to pay up," Benjamin said.

I didn't bother to comment.

"Leslie, you okay?"

"Yes," I answered, but I wasn't. My eyes were starting to swell up with those salty tears that I thought I'd sent back. I still had the anger within me to prove it.

"Want me to take you back home?"

"Yes," I answered again. I couldn't wait to get back home. **I wanted to be home more than Diana in *The Wiz*.**

"Well here we are," Benjamin said, pulling up into the empty parking space in front of my building. "Call you tomorrow?" Benjamin asked. "Oh damn, that reminds me, I'm expecting a delivery of beams tomorrow. I have to be up here by seven in the morning. I have to get a fence up for the property across the street." I watched the imaginary wheels as they turned round and round in his head.

Again, I didn't bother to answer. Was it just me, or did the fence suddenly become first priority? I wondered where I fit in on his agenda.

"Alright," I said. "I'll talk to you later."

"No kiss?" he asked, reaching for my hand before I unlocked the door.

I turned to him and gave him a little peck on the cheek.

"Goodnight," I said, leaving behind a very puzzled looking Benjamin.

I didn't hear the sound of the car's engine until I was inside the building approaching the steps. Good, he knew how I felt. And boy, was I feeling it. Hurt feelings that lasted uninterrupted through the night, spilling over into the light of the next day. Would she be back again today? What did this say about the kind of person that I was? What did it say about Benjamin? I needed a solution alright, and fast.

sista talk

"He told you what?" Rachelle asked me over a breakfast she'd made of fried whitings and grits. I had just recapped the highlights of the last evening's main events.

"Well, look at it this way," Rachelle said, crunching on the end of a cornmeal battered fishtail. "Everything you do is a risk, there's no guarantees in life, period. Don't take his reaction so negatively. Make it work to your advantage. He just might be the person you've been looking to spend the rest of your life with."

"And if he isn't?" I asked her.

"Then you go on living," she crunched and added, "and loving."

"And exactly what planet are you living on

again?" I asked her, thinking that maybe I had been a tad premature in thinking that Rachelle could totally identify with me.

"Why did I ever have to order that damn Dumpster?" I said, as I used my spoon to swirl sad faces into my plate of grits. "Anyway, enough about me, what's going on with you and Anthony?"

"Everything girl, wait a minute, are you going to eat that fish or do I have to?" Rachelle asked, reaching for my plate.

"You playin' yourself, Cuz, you know I am! There ain't that much depression in the world. Now go ahead!"

"Yeah well, I saw Anthony a little while after the hickey fight. He was real straight up. He told me his trust for me is gone, and that I would have to earn it back."

"Whaaaaat . . ." I exclaimed aloud.

"But he also said that he's not going to leave because that would be the easy way out for me. Leslie, he read me like an open book of nursery rhymes. He told me that what I went through with my whole marriage was a facade, and that I don't know what real love is."

"So did you get to explain why you had to be a sneaky, rotten, scandalous cheat?" I asked in between grit gulps.

"Sure did. He said that he'd try and find a way to help me out more. He's out looking for a better job as we speak."

"Mmph, what a twisted rarity. Better not mess that up. And what about Mr. Eustace? How's he doing?"

"Eustace's fine I guess, I haven't spoken to him since that car thing."

"So are you ever going to call him?"

"I am, but not now. I really don't miss him. Anthony is keeping me more than satisfied, thank you."

"Speak on it, Cuz."

"Damn. You weren't kidding when you said that you were going to eat your food. You finished before me," Rachelle laughed.

"Well, you were talking!"

"Whatever! But seriously, I'm glad that fighting is over. Anthony's got it goin on. Please, we be rockin and jockin all over this place!" Rachelle said, turning a shade redder than her usual tan complexion. "I'm at the height of my sexual peak and so is he! Girl, I can't wait to get it off!"

I fell out of my chair and onto the floor, laughing so hard.

"And what about you? You holding back on your favorite cousin?"

"No . . . I'm still saving that. I don't know for how much longer, but I am. Cuz I never knew how intimate a man and a woman could really be. Just the small things. A finger in the mouth, a lick of the knees . . ."

"Ahhhh! That's enough, Cuz!" Rachelle yelled out.

"No, it's just beautiful. Benjamin never tries to force me to do anything that I don't want to do, he's real affectionate."

"What's his sign?"

"Cancer."

"Yeah, Cancerians are like that."

"So you're an astrologist now?"

"I dabble in it. They also say, it's hard to do, but once you get one to fall for you, you've got their heart forever," Rachelle said, as she scooped up the last bit of grits from her plate. "I'm not giving Eustace up, you know."

"You're not?"

"Absolutely not. Eustace is different from Anthony. He's like more manly or something, and he's my back up."

"Your back up?" I asked.

"Yeah, you know, so that I'll always have someone in my life."

"That's deep, Cuz. One woman, two men—on the next Ricki Lake show."

"Men do it all the time Leslie, it's a fact of life."

"All of a sudden I don't feel so well," I said. "I think I'm just going to head back home."

"You know why you wanna head back home, don't you?" Rachelle asked me. "It's because you can't handle the truth!" Rachelle said, making us both start to laugh again before her front doorbell went off.

"Hello," Cuz said picking up the telephone to the intercom. "Okay come up, I want you to meet

my cousin anyway." Seconds later, there was a
rap at the door. Rachelle opened up the door to a
medium-height thin-framed guy who opened up
his arms to give Rachelle a giant bear hug. I gave
Anthony the once over, noticing that he was
dressed in a plain tee-shirt and oversized blue
jeans. On his head, he wore a matching blue
Knicks baseball cap, and on his feet, a pair of the
latest Nike Air sneakers. He looked like your
average all American young male, equipped with
that little bit of B-boy attitude.

"Hey, Boo, I missed you." The embrace started
to turn into something more until Anthony
looked over to see me sitting at the kitchen table.

"Anthony, this is my cousin Leslie, the one I'm
always talking to you about."

"Hey, Cuz!" Anthony exclaimed, coming over
to me and giving me a hug. "I heard a lot about
you."

"Me too," I said, returning the hug. I knew
more than he could ever think I know. The
words, *works downstairs in my lobby, little
above minimum wage*, resounding inside of my
head. To me, Anthony was average with an
above average personality.

"Do you know that I'm in love with your
cousin?" Anthony said matter-of-factly. "Did my
kids call yet?" Anthony asked, not waiting for me
to give an answer. He stood behind Rachelle with
his arms wrapped tightly around her waist. He
was referring to my little cousins. It was kind of

shocking because there's a lot of men who don't even want to take care of the kids they already have, let alone someone else's. If left up to me, Anthony had definitely passed my test. Now, all he had to do was pass Rachelle's. My guess was that it would be far from open book.

All of that lovey-dovey talk and mushy-mushy stuff was starting to make me nauseous. I was going to stay, but every time I saw Rachelle and Anthony I saw me and Benjamin. I couldn't take that anymore, so I decided to make a pleasant exit. Anyway, I didn't think Rachelle and Anthony would have too much trouble finding something to occupy their time with.

❖

A facade. A big facade was what I was putting up. I was only fooling myself until he'd telephoned that evening.

"Hey!" he said, in that cheery way that only he could say it.

"Hey, yourself," I answered in a less than enthusiastic tone.

"How've you been?" he asked.

"As well as can be expected," I answered calmly.

"What does that mean?"

"It means I'm okay, Benjamin."

"Well it sure doesn't sound like it to me."

"So why did you ask?" I said, feeling my nostrils flare open.

"Look Leslie, I'm not going to argue with you. I had enough of that with my ex-wife."

"Excuse you? Did you say ex-wife?"

"Didn't I tell you?"

No you didn't tell me, I thought. **I would have been sure to have remembered an ex-wife.**

"I was married for four years," he went on to say. "She tried to control me. What I said, the things I did. All of a sudden I was changing. I was changing into the person she wanted me to be. Everything was a fight, I couldn't take all of that aggravation."

"Well what did she argue about?" I asked him. I was curious about what he would say. Besides, it doesn't take a genius to figure out that there are two sides to a story.

"Little things, her own insecurities."

"Okay . . . remember to remind me to ask you more about your ex-marriage, and your ex-wife later." I wasn't about to push the subject, just yet.

"I miss you, you know. Leslie, I want to see you."

"Did you stop working on the block?"

"No, I still am, but lately I've been taking on a lot of outside contracting work so that I can finance my own inside projects. I'm thinking about opening a business close by. One-hundred-and-forty-fifth street."

"That's good." No wonder I had fallen for this man. He was so ambitious, always ready to make a move.

"Please, can I come see you just for a little while? Can't we try to work this out?" he pleaded.

"You make it sound so easy. Go ahead and give it a try. I'd like to see how you plan on straightening this one out so quick," I said, taking a gamble against my own better judgment. "But Benjamin, only for a little while. I mean it."

"I'm on my way over."

Forty-five minutes later he was there, and looking as good as ever, undeniably happy to see me. We sat on the carpet and talked as I took on the role of ready-made therapist.

"So tell me, Benjamin, why are you so unhappy with her? I'm talking about your live-in girlfriend or your common-law wife, whichever you prefer to refer to her as being," I said, getting right down to it.

"You don't waste any time getting to the point, do you?"

"Not where my heart is concerned." Benjamin grabbed a blue throw pillow from off of the couch and placed it behind his head to lay back. I took a vertical position on the floor next to him, laying the back of my head on top of his very cushiony stomach.

"I don't know why I'm unhappy with her."

"I mean you must have been happy with her at one time or another."

"In the beginning, I was . . ." he said, stroking my hair from front to back in smooth, even motions. It was making me uncomfortable. *Don't stroke my hair while you're reminiscing about her.* That's what I thought to myself. Of course I didn't tell him that.

"And then things just started to fall apart. I was finding myself away from her a lot of the time. We just grew out of each other I think."

"Well it takes two, are you even trying to make things work?"

"Believe me I've tried, but the sparks just aren't there anymore," he said.

"Have you told her this?" I asked, shifting my head to look Benjamin in the face.

"Yes."

"So what did she say?"

"Nothing much. I told her that I was unhappy and that was that."

There had to be more to it than that, I thought to myself, turning my head away, but once again, I wasn't going to stress that now. Of course I knew that there were two sides to a story. He could just be telling me what I want to hear. Whatever the case, it was working for now. It was working until I could get confirmation or something more substantial. Only time would tell. At least the lines of communication had been opened. It was the start of something, which made it easier to stare at Benjamin. Something I never felt comfortable doing before. If he was gonna look into the depths of my soul, I was gonna look into his too. The mellow sounds of Brian McKnight serenaded softly in the background and our only light source came from the blue neon fluorescent telephone I had just purchased and hung on the wall. The ambiance was most definitely in effect. We started touching each other. Feeling, kissing . . . and then, I stopped him. Benjamin didn't know I was a twenty-one-year-old virgin, and besides that, the timing felt all wrong. If I were to tell him now, he'd only pursue me harder, and I wasn't sure if I wanted that. Not yet.

"What's the matter?" Benjamin asked.

"We need to slow down, that's all."

"That's not a big problem Leslie. You'll find that I have a lot of patience," he told me, embracing me as we lay on the carpet listening to music. Just as we'd started out.

rachelle: sixth sense

◈: oh damn this is good! Yes! Whose is this?" Eustace yelled out from over the top of Rachelle. She needn't have bothered to reply. It was obvious that he had been having enough fun for both of them. She couldn't help but to wish she was with Anthony.

"I'm coming!!! Ohhhhh!" Eustace cried out loudly, giving Rachelle a kiss on the cheek, rolling over, and then getting up to take a quick shower. That was it.

Rachelle lay in bed wondering exactly what the hell she was doing in a hotel with Eustace. She thought hard. She was there because . . . She was there because . . . Damnit! Why couldn't she get past that part? It just wasn't like her to be at a loss for words. In a few minutes, he'd be leaving her to go home to his family. It was bad enough that she had lied her way out of the house. It had been simple enough to concoct a lame story about her hanging out with Leslie. All that, and for what? Anthony deserved better.

Eustace came out all dressed, clothes without a wrinkle. No signs of an affair. Why was it that she was always the one having to cover her ass? And here he was all ready to go? She suddenly hopped up from out of the bed with the sheet wrapped around her. Eustace thought he was who? Shoot, he wasn't the only one with a life and a family to go home to.

"Okay Sweetie, call me tomorrow at the store," Eustace said, giving Rachelle a kiss on the lips, skimming her shoulders with his hands.

"Don't start anything that you can't finish!" Rachelle joked, knowing very well that inside she was serious. And he stopped touching. "Yeah, you know exactly what the deal is!"

Eustace just stood there grinning from ear to ear, adding a smug, "Don't forget to call me at the store!"

"Where else would I call you at, Eustace?" Rachelle said, pulling the sheet in tighter around her body, shielding her nakedness behind the semi-closed door. "I can't very well call you at home now, can I?"

"Real funny, Rachelle," Eustace replied, snatching up his car keys and slipping out the door, not forgetting to give Rachelle one last loving wink.

"What the hell does he care?" Rachelle asked staring at the pile of her clothes that were left to lie on the floor. Dammit, they were all wrinkled.

Rachelle turned the key quietly in its lock, slipped out of her shoes, and tiptoed quietly inside so as to not awaken anyone. Anthony and the kids were all knocked out asleep on the couch. The dishes had been washed, the kitchen was spotless, and everything was in its place. The house looked better than the way she had left it. Guilt was a mother. "My life's all fucked up," Rachelle said softly, picking up each kid and putting them in the bed of their own room. Then she showered and slipped on a nightgown, snuggling up near a warm bodied Anthony on the couch.

Anthony sleepily turned over to face Rachelle and said, "Goodnight Boo, love you."

"I love you too, Anthony," Rachelle answered. It was exactly what she needed to hear.

Bright and early, up with the kids, Rachelle was readily dishing up homemade waffles and sausage for everybody. The kids were watching their usual early Saturday morning cartoons, and Anthony was still sleeping. Well, at least he was.

"Good-morning," a groggy-eyed Anthony told Rachelle, shuffling into the kitchen like one of her own children.

"Hey sleepy head," Rachelle answered, pouring another batch of pancake batter into the hot waffle iron. The sizzle of the batter against the hot metal grid served as a comfort to her each time a new set went in.

"Mmmm, homemade waffles, turkey bacon, and sausage? What did I do to deserve all this?"

"Just being you, that's what, and I couldn't ask for anything more."

"Aww! That's so sweet!" Anthony joked. "Now pass me a plate, Boo, I'm starving." Rachelle served Anthony up a heaping mansize breakfast and an ice cold glass of orange juice.

"Kids come eat!" Tyreek, Zoie, and Jaree came running into the kitchen.

"Ma, I'm hungry!" little Tyreek shouted out, clinging onto Rachelle's leg.

"Boy, go sit down before something hot falls on you!"

"How?" Tyreek asked looking up wide-eyed at his mother.

"Just go sit down, and mommy will take care of you." Tyreek flashed a big toothy smile to his mother.

"I'm the man of the house right, Ma?" Tyreek asked.

"Yes, yes you are. You know that," Rachelle answered. Then she served up three more plates of breakfast and made sure that all of her kids were seated and happy. She looked over at the table, at Anthony and the kids eating. Her little family, she loved them so much. Now this was the way things were supposed to be.

"Come eat with us, Rachelle."

"I'm coming," Rachelle said, going over to the kitchen table. It was times like this that made her feel like the black June Cleaver, wanting everything to be just so. The kids were getting maple syrup everywhere, but she really didn't care just as long as they were enjoying their breakfast.

"Rachelle?"

"Huh?" Rachelle answered, peeling the sides off her bacon.

"I know that you got in here real late last night. You don't have to tell me where you were."

"Excuse me, do you kids want to watch TV in the other room while you eat?"

"Yeah!" all three shouted out.

"Anthony, could you please move the kids' table into the living room?"

"No problem."

"Now you were saying?" Rachelle asked, continuing to eat only after the kids had gone into the other room.

"Yeah, I was saying," Anthony continued, "after that hickey thing it's kind of hard to trust you."

"What's a relationship without trust Anthony? You've got to trust that I'll do the right thing. Anybody can make a mistake, being only human."

"In answer to your question, a relationship without trust is a fucked up one that won't last too long."

"And you're saying all this to say what Anthony? Are you threatening me?"

"No, I'm not. Let me make myself clear, this is not an argument. What I'm saying is, I see that your car is working better than ever."

"Spit it out, Anthony, say what it is you wanna say!" She wasn't quite sure how to handle this one.

"Well, the bottom line is that I don't make a lot of money, and I know that you have financial needs. Right now I can't handle all of them. Shit, I can't even handle half of them. I know that you have to do what you have to do, and I know that in the end, it's me that you'll come home to. You wanna say anything, Boo?"

"No." Rachelle said, dropping her fork onto her plate of cold breakfast. What else was there to say? Anthony had said it all and it was scary to hear him say exactly what she was thinking.

just anotha' day

As my college professor proceeded to wrap up his lecture, I let my mind wander off to the night before with Benjamin. 2:00 a.m. and nothing happened. That's the time he left, and part of me hated to see him leave. I wondered if he'd ever stay the whole night. Well he'd have to, if he had any intentions of being with me. I wondered what that woman said when he came in the house at that time. Didn't she even care? Couldn't be me, I thought.

"Ms. Williams . . . Ms. Williams . . . Ms. Williams!"

"Oh, yes Professor Ivers?" I snapped out of my daze and answered. How long had she been calling my name?

"Please, continue to pass copies of the research paper outline down!"

"Oh, sorry!" I replied. "I didn't hear you."

"Apparently not, Ms. Williams!" Echoes of laughter filled the room. I hated this class, it was soooo boring. Who cared about anthropology anyway?

"Wake up!" Kenny said, as he leaned over my desk and shouted in my ear. Kenny's this crazy cool gay guy in my class. He usually keeps me amused during my hour and a half of torture.

"That's my ears you're yelling into!"

"Then stop daydreaming about that man, girl."

"What?"

"I said, stop daydreaming about that man. I know you are because you've got that faraway look in your eyes."

"I do?" I said, taking out my compact mirror to stare at my reflection.

"I look the same to me." I knew better, I was just playing along to pass the time. At this point, anything would work.

"You can't see it, you silly rabbit, it's only detectable by another human eye. And you have got it bad, girlfriend."

"Listen, I don't know about all that Mr. Kenny, but I do know that it is time to get outta here." Benjamin was coming to pick me up. We were going to catch a play, and I couldn't wait to leave.

After class let out, I walked downstairs, and

outside into the bright warmth of the daylight. The intensity of the sun's rays felt good against my face. It was a good change compared to the frigid air-conditioned classroom that I had been in all day. I was looking along the street curb for the burgundy colored Saab that I knew belonged to my guy, when I suddenly spotted it. No sooner had he spotted me and started to beep his horn than I flashed a wide smile and gave a big wave hello heading towards the car.

"Hey," he said, giving me a warm kiss as I got inside the car.

"Hey yourself."

"You look good," he said, giving me the once over.

I had made a point to look especially cute today, knowing that he was coming to pick me up. "Yeah, tell me anything," I laughed.

"You just can't take a compliment can you? Women! I bet if I stopped complimenting, you'd start complaining. You never notice anything about me, you don't love me anymore," he mocked.

"Okay fine, thank you. Thank you for the compliments honey, but don't give them all to me now, and not bother to give any later."

"Oh I don't think you'll have to worry about that, cause I'm going to be complimenting you even when you're old and gray," he said. I was rendered speechless. The future-tense thing was a keeper. We saw the play *The Lion King*, did the dinner thing, and were heading back to my house.

Benjamin parked the car and we walked to my building hand in hand, and of course all of the natives were out, and very restless. All of the men seemed to want to stop and ask questions about work, and all of the women just smiled and waved, waved and smiled. It was enough to make me sick to my stomach. I'm remembering this one older woman in particular who had yelled out,

"Benjamin be careful, a minor's a terrible thing to waste!"

Benjamin went over there and put her in her place. I was pretty glad about that, because if he hadn't I sure would have. What I was not so glad about was all the extra attention this relationship was getting. All the rumors and things, it was really getting to me. Some of which were, the wife is looking for me, he always keeps young girls on the side, and just a bunch of bull to make me upset.

"I keep telling you honey, don't let these people get to you," Benjamin told me, as we walked up the steps inside of my building. "People are going to talk regardless. None of them are paying your rent, or paying any of your bills, right?"

"Right. I know I shouldn't let these people get to me, I'm a very private person. Do you or don't you even mind if people are always up in our business?"

"Don't."

"Maybe you should, kissing and hugging all over me openly in the street like you do. And what if she pops up to see you, and we're kissing or something?"

"If that's what's meant to happen, then it just will."

"Please, Benjamin."

"Why do you ask me a question, if you're only gonna turn around and answer it yourself? I mean, what else can I do? If she pops up, as you call it, then I'll just excuse myself and go and try to explain the situation to her."

"And pray tell, what is the situation?" I asked, as we walked inside my apartment. I went to the refrigerator, got us two cold drinks, and we went inside the bedroom to lie across the bed.

"You don't know?" he asked.

"I'm not certain."

"The situation, which I certainly didn't plan on, is that I'm in love with you Leslie. I am **in love with you, Leslie Williams.**"

It was those three killer words. Words I had anticipated and prepared myself for. Words that I would not let go to my head before knowing the true sincerity behind their meaning, transcending it into more than mere words. And then we kissed. I think I loved his kissing more than he loved mine, but I'd never tell him that. I would also never tell him that the feeling was mutual. Telling him I loved him would be a big mistake.

Tell a man you love him too fast, and they start running straight in the opposite direction. They start to catch the commitment confusion, I call it. But now he was kissing me, my eyes, my ears, and the most sensitive spots of my neck. He slowly unbuttoned my shirt and started to lick me from the top of my head to the tips of my toes. Yeah, you heard right, I couldn't believe it either. I'd never let a man get so close to me, physically or emotionally. I started to moan, he got up on top of me and started moving. I managed to muffle out a small stop, hardly convincing. I was enticed, feeling his hardness rubbing against the inside of my thighs.

"Stop . . ."

"Why?" . . . he asked still doing what he was doing.

Because I'm a virgin. *Psyche*. I didn't tell him that yet, it was really more like, "Stop. I'm not ready."

"Yes you are . . . your body is telling me that you are . . ."

"But my head is not."

He rolled over and stopped.

"You upset?" I asked him.

"No, I told you I have a lot of patience," he replied, placing both hands behind his head. "I'll wait for you for as long as I have to." He took me into his arms again and gave me a big hug, and we fell asleep right in each other's embrace. He left after eleven, almost minutes to twelve. He was starting to stay longer and longer. For some reason, I was starting to feel more secure with a man who was probably making another woman feel just the reverse.

love is

"So what street is Magdalena's on?" Rachelle asked me as we sped off down the street in her small blue compact Toyota.

"It's on a hundred and fifty-third and Broadway."

"Oh-okay, I was thinking one fiftieth."

"No, that's Lusette's shop over there. Trust me, that is not where you want to go. I've heard quite a few horror stories about that place," I told Rachelle.

"Horror stories like what?"

"Like try no hot water, bad haircuts, and three hairdressers to a head."

"Three people?"

"You heard me, all at once. Don't worry," I laughed, "Magdalena's is nothing like that."

Magdalena's is the hot spot to get your hair done. For $18, a stylist would hook your hair up in a fresh done wash, set, and blow or the wrap, as most females called it.

"You're getting your hair wrapped right?" Rachelle asked.

"Yeah, and I've got the pins to prove it, see?" I said, holding the pack up in front of me. "I'll probably get my ends clipped too. What are you getting?"

"A wash and blow, then I'll let them put some of those neat little hot curls in. I'm gonna try something new for a change."

"Girl, my hair is screaming for a relaxer," I said. "I can barely run a comb through it. So, how's everything else going with you and your mens?"

"Did you say something Cuz?" Rachelle asked.

"Anthony, Eustace. Earth to Rachelle . . . are you still with me?"

"Yeah I'm fine," she said. "No I'm not fine! Must you notice every damn thing?"

"Mmhm, it's my job, now make a right here. Besides, who else is gonna do it?"

"Alright the lowdown is that Anthony's fine, I met his mom and his sister. Anthony must look like his father because I don't see any of his mother in him. They're cool though. They've helped me out with the kids and everything.

Feels just like family, and I've only known them for a couple of weeks. And Anthony? No complaints. He's good to me, certainly, the best lover I've ever had. He makes me feel whole . . . always taking his time and going all out to make sure that I'm satisfied. Last week he tells me that I can see other people because he knows that he can't give me everything that I want or need. And check this out, he also said that he's not going to see anyone outside of our relationship, he'll remain totally dedicated to me and only me."

"Whaaat?" I said, as I jerked my head back into the headrest of the car. "So what's the problem?" I asked sarcastically.

"The problem is, what am I doing in a serious relationship with a twenty-one-year-old? I can't continue to go on like this. I've got three kids, Leslie."

"Well what about Eustace?" I asked.

"What about him? Eustace has a wife and kids," Rachelle answered. "He's calling me twenty-four-seven, and I know why . . ."

Rachelle answered before I ever could.

"It's because he thinks that I'm seeing someone else."

"But you are Cuz," I told her.

"Yes, but Eustace doesn't know that for sure. But he senses it Leslie. He doesn't really want me."

"Well do you really want him?" I asked.

"Yes, but not in the way that you think. I want

Eustace to really want me for me, I mean really want me for me. Then he can go back to his wife and kids because I wouldn't want him then."

"That's deep Cuz," I told her. "Maybe you just don't want anybody right now. I mean you're just getting out of a ten-year marriage, and you're finally getting to explore your own independence."

"I know you're right Leslie, but does that mean that in the process I can't have a man to love and for him to love me back?"

"Now love, that's a word you can't use lightly. People abuse it all the time. Oh I love you, but if you loved me, love you . . . but then they just turn around and do different shit. If you really loved me, then you wouldn't be doing the things that you do, that's what it's really about. You know that saying, Men give love for sex, and women give sex for love?"

"Yeah," Rachelle answered.

"For some odd reason that saying stays in my mind."

"Well just don't let it mess up your relationship with Benjamin."

"No, I'm not. He told me he loved me, you know."

"Whaat? When?"

"Last week, except I'm trying not to get my hopes all up and about."

"I'd say that was a good sign, Cuz. You know Anthony tells me that he loves me constantly, too bad love don't pay the bills. At least your man is his own boss, and has access to money."

"That's not why I'm in the relationship Rachelle."

"Who said that it was? Now Eustace has his own business. Why can't Anthony be Eustace? Isn't that Magdalena's on the next block?" Rachelle asked, after eyeing the red and black facade of the shop.

"Yeah, that's it," I said. "It sounds like you'd like a combination of both men to me." We pulled up into an empty parking spot right in front of the salon.

"Good timing," Rachelle said, putting the car into Park.

"Don't speak too fast. Look inside of that shop, it's overflowing."

We locked the car and went inside. It was overflowing alright, like a tub of running water. As we walked inside, and past the row of women underneath the clear huge bubbled hair dryers, all eyes were upon us. I led the way, heading straight towards the back where the sinks were. "This is where we get washed and conditioned," I whispered over to Rachelle. The back of the shop was just as crowded as the front. There was a line, seemingly infinite, which consisted of a long row of heads, lined up much like that of wooden toy soldiers.

I had to try and find a new salon. Magdalena's had become far too fashionable. Literally everyone and their mother had started to go there. There had to be somebody else in Manhattan that could do a presentable hair fix. Rachelle and I found two seats in the far corner in back of the salon. We both looked and listened in on the idle chatter and gossip that buzzed around us. Just then a short, thin-framed girl came into the back of the salon, asking for Fifi, the head beautician.

"Excuse me, how much would it cost for a wash and set?"

"It's $18, but you can't get that! When was the last time you had a perm?" Fifi asked in her heavy native Dominican accent.

"About two weeks ago," the girl answered in a soft-spoken tone, touching her own hair as if she herself was unsure.

Fifi grabbed the girl's tangled hair roughly and said, "No we can't do that! You need a perm! $40!" Out of nowhere the small scenario had turned into a spotlighted showcase because everyone in the back of the salon was glaring at the poor young girl who only wanted to know how much a wash and set was.

"Well then I guess I won't be getting my hair done here because I don't have enough money on me."

OUTCAST! STONE HER! FREAK! These words were not said, but implied by Fifi and her spectators. The girl left the salon head down, almost in shame.

"That don't make no sense," Rachelle said after the girl had walked out of the shop.

"That was uncalled for," I added. "You wanna leave, Cuz?"

"No child, I'm gettin my hair done today, I brought enough money!"

We laughed to ourselves until a chair at one of the sinks became available. First I went, then Cuz. We stayed in that salon for two hours, but like I said, when we left our hair was jumpin. Fifi had done it again.

nightmare on "my" street

had a bizarre nightmare last night. I dreamt that Sonia found out about me. *She was after me on a hunt, like a game man in pursuit of its prey and I was to be the next prize on her mantel. There was a heavy stench of death thick in the air, leaving behind a trail that would imminently lead her and her gun straight to me. I was running and running on down that path of no return, moving so rapidly that it hadn't felt like I'd had any legs to run with. But the faster I ran, the closer she got. I fled into this dark, dead end. Everything was pitch dark, but I was seeing silver. Silver in the eerie way that the 45 caliber's smooth exterior gleamed, underneath the moon's rays. In relation to distance, she must have been directly in front of me, unflinching, with the gun held steady, clasped tightly between both of her hands. There was nowhere else to run. Yes, I was trapped. I stared down into the endless bluck hole of the barrel, and my impending doom . . . She had me, and said that she wouldn't kill me if I could give her one, just one good reason for taking her man of six years. The man she had made a home for, cooked, cleaned, and loved with every fiber of her own being. Joint bank accounts, ups and downs, ins and outs. She had been the one there for him through it all.*

"Give me one reason not to shoot a bullet through one side of your head and out the other!" she demanded.

I opened my mouth, but no words would come out. She cocked the gun as I struggled for words that came out in the form of quick gasps, each being shorter than the one before. She pulled the trigger. There was a thunderous sound. The gun went off.

I woke up in a cold sweat, relieved that it had only been a dream. I got up from out of my bed, the covers of which had been strewn across the floor, and went to make some warm milk. I returned, and sat on the edge of the bed. I could feel myself trembling. It was only 9:30 a.m., and a Saturday, but I knew that there was no way I could go back to sleep. How far from reality was this nightmare? Something like that could really happen but strangely, fear wasn't the emotion I was feeling. The guilt alone had been enough. If he cheated on her, he could just as easily do it to me. And he lives a lie. I'm sure that he's lying to her. Telling her he's doing something else when he's really with me. Six years is a long time to be involved with somebody. Even if they're not married, there's still that certain amount of commitment involved. He told me that she does love him. And to have one person suddenly take all that away. . . . No, let me change that. I do feel fear. Fear that what goes around comes around. But I couldn't just walk away. Not just like that, I thought, taking a sip of the overheated microwaved milk in my mug. I was in too deep.

Ring, ring! The sound of the phone startled me, causing me to spill half the cup of hot milk on my legs.

"Hello!" I blurted out.

"You alright?"

"Yeah, I'm fine. I just spilled some milk, that's all," I said, rubbing the burning spot above my knees.

"Are you dressed?" It was Benjamin. "I want you to come downstairs and meet my son."

"Your son? I mean, okay." I was dumbfounded, and I couldn't blame it on the spilt milk.

"Okay, I'll meet you downstairs in say, twenty minutes?"

"Alright, bye," I said as I hung up the phone.

Was he crazy? Was I crazy? Meet his son? His son's all of thirteen years old! Then I'm thinking, why not? People are out there in the world meeting new people all the time. What's the big deal? He wants me to meet his son, well okay then, I'll meet his son.

I got dressed and went downstairs. I saw the car, but no one was in it. Benjamin was working on a church on the block, so I went inside to see if maybe they were in there. A workman was the only one inside. He was laying some redwood parquet onto the church floor.

"Have you seen Benjamin?" I asked him.

"Yeah, he's across the street in the lot with his son, and Sam."

I'd never paid any attention to the lot before, which is odd because I've lived on this block for almost 4 years now. I went through the opening in the fence. Although I was walking through it, I was feeling every bit apprehensive about it. The whole going through the fence thing, I mean. No, that wasn't quite it. I mean, suppose his son didn't like me? A better question to ask myself was just what was I walking into anyway? I followed a narrow dirt path which led to a small existent basketball court where Benjamin, his son, and his partner Sam were shooting hoops.

Once I was completely inside, I stood there. I stood right there in my spot almost paralyzed, but did manage to muster up a painted smile reminiscent of the one Mona Lisa sported in her portrait.

"You're cheatin', Pop!" his son yelled out as he held both of his arms up.

God, they resembled one another. The stance, the defined facial features, the big mouth . . .

"No, you're just a sore loser!" Benjamin shouted back. It was basketball-lingo defense at its best. I could tell that they were close. It was cute, seeing father and son like that. After about fifteen minutes of ball, they quit. Benjamin came over and introduced his son to me.

"Kareem this is Leslie, Leslie this is Kareem," he said, walking on ahead of us with Sam.

This was the moment I had dreaded. Left alone to talk with Kareem. What would I say? Maybe I'd try. . . . *So, do you think I look anything like a mistress should look? Oh no wait, even better; You look just like your mother, how is she anyway?* I amused myself at the thought, and proceeded to take the safer route. Sports.

"You like Michael Jordan?"

"Naah!" he answered.

"So, who's your favorite basketball player?"

"Clyde Drexler," he answered.

"Yeah? How old are you?"

"Thirteen," he smiled. I smiled back, then I gave him the big double nod.

And that was the gist of our conversation. We climbed back through the hole in the gate, back onto the block. The lemonade man was out there and Benjamin bought styrofoam cups full for everybody. I politely declined, telling Benjamin that I had something else to do. "It was nice meeting you Kareem, and I'll talk to you later Benjamin." Well that went well, I mumbled under my breath as I headed back upstairs.

Then it dawned on me, I had just met my boyfriend's son. But why would he do that? I questioned. Maybe I had better put a lid on all of my budding happiness. It was one thing to know Benjamin had thought I was special enough to meet his son, but the son could easily go back and tell his mother. I mean, we didn't kiss or anything, but then again why would his father just introduce this strange young woman to him? The side spectator from nowhere? I don't think so. Kids ain't stupid. This just isn't adding up to me. Then again, maybe I'm not supposed to add. Maybe I should be subtracting. Better yet even, I think I will divide.

❖

I wound up spending the rest of the day studying. I had a history exam in a few days and I wanted to ace it because my grades had started to slip on account of the stress from the work I was doing on the building. Later on that evening, Benjamin called me.

"Hey hon," he said.

"Hi."

"So?"

"So what?" I asked.

"So what did you think of my son?"

"Oh I like him. He's real handsome. I know he'll be a real lady killer when he gets older," I said.

"Shucks, all that boy thinks about is sports. He's a diehard basketball fan."

"But that's natural at his age, that's why I said when he gets older. Come to the realization Benjamin, at some point in his life Kareem will begin to show an interest in girls."

"Don't remind me," Benjamin laughed.

Being that we were on the subject of Kareem, I decided to ask, "Benjamin, what made you do it? What made you introduce me to Kareem?"

"Well I felt that it was time for two people that I care very much for to meet each other. Didn't you want to meet him?"

"Yeah, I'm sayin, I'm glad we met. Just with the situation being what it is, I thought it might be awkward."

"Awkward?"

"Yes awkward."

"Did you feel awkward?" he asked me.

"No, not really."

"Good. Then when things start to feel awkward I'll just have to deal with it, that's all."

The silence on the telephone line was deafening.

"Leslie, are you still there?"

a wonderful life

Rachelle rolled out of her bed, literally springing to her feet to get a jump start on the long day that she knew lay ahead. First things first, the proper attire. Tyreek and Jaree could wear their navy blue suits with their unworn, still-with-the-tag-on white dress shirts she'd purchased over two months ago. Zoie could wear her new pastel blue floral dress with the black ruffle trim. Some Shirley Temple curls in Zoie's hair would add just the right touch. Everything had to be perfect. This was after all, Zoie's very special day.

Today, Zoie would receive her art award from her creative arts class. Besides receiving a certificate, Zoie would also be getting a $50 savings bond to be put towards her future educational expenses. Rachelle was so proud. With three children to put through college, every penny counted, and any scholarships or awards they received was a definite plus. For herself, Rachelle set out her white two-piece linen pantsuit. Good, everything was all set. Now all she had to do was find those tickets . . . It would be a shame to have been so well prepared and not even able to get into the damn award ceremony. Oh yes, on top of the refrigerator, she remembered. She had put them in an envelope on top of the refrigerator. Rachelle grabbed the envelope up quickly, carefully counting out the four orange tickets inside.

"One for myself, one for my mother, one for Cuz, and one for . . ."

Rachelle wouldn't permit her mind to go all the way there. Initially, the ticket belonged to Anthony, who by the way, had been acting strangely ever since that last it's-me-you'll-come-home-to-Boo conversation. He was beginning to stay at his aunt's house more often, and he definitely wasn't calling as much. As a matter of fact, Rachelle couldn't even remember the last time he had called. She just couldn't understand it because she'd been on her best behavior lately, which meant no contact with Eustace or any other potential home-lover-friends of hers. Shit, Anthony wasn't even giving her the benefit of the doubt. And what brought on the sudden change of heart? Because Rachelle was finally starting to realize that she was number one, that she deserved the best, and that the man who went all out for her was the man she needed to have in her life. That man was Anthony, hands down.

The award ceremony was a little longer than Rachelle had expected, running over its original one hour time slot, but it was worth it. Seeing her baby happy and all was good enough for her, Zoie could do no wrong that day.

The event was held outside in the garden pavilion. Millions of blades of green grass and white plastic lawn chairs spread evenly throughout. The weather was sunny and bright. We sat right up front, so that we wouldn't miss anything. And when they called Zoie Mason we all stood up, clapped and yelled as loud as we could, little Zoie looked a little embarrassed. The whole event was being captured on videotape "a la Rachelle style." That meant mostly close-ups and blur, but nonetheless the event was timeless. I volunteered the use of my video services, but Rachelle insisted that she knew how to work her own camcorder. Another aesthetically wonderful video to add to her collection.

Rachelle tucked all three of her little ones snugly into their beds. She couldn't help but to stand over them looking down to admire their cute little faces. At least their father had done one thing right, Rachelle thought, smiling to herself. They were growing up so fast, too fast. It would only be a matter of time before they were off to college and out of the house. She had never anticipated such a feeling of loneliness in all her life because for the most part, she had always remembered having someone there for her. And it wasn't the kids that gave her this feeling. No, they were very much a big part of her existence. But deep, deep down inside she knew that the empty loneliness she felt stemmed from the absence of Anthony. He knew that today was Zoie's award ceremony, yet he hadn't even bothered to call. Her answering machine could attest to that. Anthony always said that no matter what happened to them that he would always be there for the kids. What a joke! What Anthony was doing made no sense at all. Was this the price one had to pay for falling in love? Every day was becoming an obstacle, and the nights? The nights were long and lonely.

Where was this man when she was ready to give her heart? Probably with another, Rachelle thought, turning the dimmer down in the kid's room. Zoie was afraid of the dark. Rachelle was afraid of being alone. Being alone meant no one to help share the bills. Rent, telephone, cable for the kids, insurance premiums, utilities . . . Being alone meant that she'd have a harder time raising her sons. Who would be there as a male role model to set the example of what being a man was all about? They needed to know that a man should always respect a woman and what holding their own really meant. Had she succeeded with them thus far?

Sure, she could tell them what to do at the young ages of 6 and 8, but what would happen when they were older? And being alone meant no stolen kisses or late night loving. The truth of the matter was, Zoie would outgrow her fears, but when would she? There was only one thing left to do.

❖

The steaming hot angular beams of water felt good gushing down against my arms, neck, and back. Clouds of thick misty steam had transformed my bathroom into a mini-sauna. After my shower, I decided to treat myself to a quickie aloe facial mask. Enjoying the new smoothness of my skin, I left my hair up in the French roll it had been done up in, only set off with tapered bangs in front. I slipped into my favorite Ann Taylor shirt, and taupe catsuit. Benjamin would be over any minute now, **with news.** I wondered what kind of news it was, immediately assuming the worst. Maybe he was coming over to tell me that it was over between us, or just maybe he'd left her. . . . My thoughts were interrupted by a sudden knock at the door. As I peered through the peephole I realized that I was not too far from finding out.

"Mmph, I missed you so much," Benjamin said, giving me a big bear hug and kiss after I had opened the door.

"Hey handsome, get on in here," I said, fighting back the urge to say I missed him too. Benjamin was dressed in a velour navy blue jogging suit and white running shoes.

"So what were you doing?" he asked me.

"Nothing much, just trying to clean up a little before you came," I said, fluffing up the two Kente style pillows, and taking a seat next to Benjamin on the couch.

"You look nice. But then you always do," he told me.

"Thanks. Okay, now get to the news you have to tell me," I said in an overanxious tone.

"What?" Benjamin said aloud to the television, suddenly engrossed in an episode of America's Most Wanted. "That's crazy," he added, "that could never happen if he was here in New York!"

Well I was in New York, and it wasn't doing me a bit of good. I was being ignored.

"I'm sorry honey. Now what were you saying?"

"The news?" I asked him again.

"Oh it's nothing. I'm leaving to go to Atlanta for a week or so, so I won't see you for a while."

"Oh," I said. *Well was that all? Wait, what was I thinking about? Then I'm wondering . . .*

"Who are you going with?" *Curiosity killed the cat . . .*

"My son and his mother." *Satisfaction brought*

him back . . . "Why do you do that?" I asked him in an irate tone. "My son and his mother, you say it like she's not connected with you. Just stop it!"

"Fine," he answered.

"So it's a vacation sort of thing?" I asked, deliberately avoiding eye contact, looking down at the rug on the floor.

"Yeah, sort of. Look Leslie, I'm only trying to be honest with you. In fact, the truth is that it would have been easier for me to have made up a lie. Would you have wanted that?"

"Maybe," I answered. "Maybe you should have lied." What was I saying? "No, no you don't need to lie to me. You know, this relationship is getting harder and harder to deal with. I mean, is this going away with your family thing supposed to be something I'm just supposed to get used to?"

"No Leslie, but you do have to expect things like this to happen. Nobody said that this would be smooth sailing straight through."

"How am I supposed to expect things that I've never experienced before? Try to remember that this isn't the norm for me either, Benjamin. What I need right now is honesty. Just tell me, do you really want to be in this relationship with me? I mean, is this what you want?"

Benjamin turned his head and sighed. "Would I be here if I didn't?"

"I don't know, you tell me."

"I'm trying to. Leslie, I'm in love with you. I don't plan on going anywhere." Benjamin moved in closer and gave me a hug. "Now does that answer your question?" I responded with a hug back, which turned into a kiss. A kiss turned into light petting, light petting turned into foreplay. Very enjoyable foreplay that I had to interrupt Benjamin right in the middle of, again.

"What's wrong Leslie? Why is it that you always stop me here?"

"Benjamin, I have something to tell you."

"You told me that the last time, but you never said what it was."

"I know, it's just not one of those things that you can just say . . ." I said, sitting up on the couch and buttoning my shirt.

"Okay, should I try to guess what it is?"

I shook my head up down in agreement.

"You always stop me before our lovemaking gets too heavy for you so it has to have something to do with that. Were you ever abused?"

"No!" I blurted out. "Where would you get that from? Oh just forget it, you'll never figure it out." *You'll never figure out that I'm a virgin Benjamin.* "I'm a virgin," I repeated, for the second time in a tone which was more audible than the first.

"Say what?" Benjamin asked.

Had he stopped breathing? His face turned a bright crimson, and his mouth hung wide open. As open and as prolonged as a tunnel, on both ends. At first it was funny, seeing his face make an expression like that. I couldn't help but to laugh.

"You're joking right?"

My smile took a turn for the worst. Why would I be joking about something as important as this? "No, I am not joking."

"You know it all makes sense now."

"What are you talking about?"

"You . . . Whenever I asked you sexual questions or made sexual advances, just your responses, that's all."

"So that leads you to think what?" I asked.

"I'm thinking that it's wonderful. It's wonderful to have found a young woman who respects her body enough to wait for the right person. But why did you wait so long to tell me?"

"I didn't know how. I wanted the timing to be right."

"So you never even came close to doing it?"

"Not really, just light petting."

"That's all? All of this time? Honey, that's wonderful," Benjamin said, showering me with a trail of kisses across my forehead.

"Can you stop saying that, it's wonderful, it's wonderful!"

"But it is, honey, don't you think so?"

"Yes I do, but don't make me out to be the Virgin Mary or anything. I'm no martyr, Benjamin." *It's wonderful, it's wonderful*, he'd stopped saying it, but I knew he was still thinking it. I tried changing the subject. "So when are you leaving for Atlanta? Benjamin, did you hear me?" No doubt about it, he was still in shock because his mouth hadn't closed all the way yet. Good thing there were no flies around. I know, I know, don't tell me, it's wonderful right?

been there, done that

It was raining cats and dogs on that particular Sunday. I'd stayed over at Rachelle's house because she'd said that she had something real important to do. For some odd reason, she wouldn't tell me what it was, though. It was early, about 9:30 a.m. The kids were still asleep, on account of us letting them stay up extra late the night before to pop popcorn, watch videos, and dance around to music CDs. It's a small miracle that I'm even awake now to talk about it. I'm not the only one. I can hear the sounds of Rachelle's broken voice on the phone in the other room. It really is too bad that she never has caught on to the fine art of whispering.

"So ten o'clock, I'll be there. Yeah, in front of

your building. I'll be driving a blue Pontiac. Okay bye," Rachelle said on the telephone, as she passed through the living room on route to the bathroom. She'd neglected to notice that I was sitting up looking at her from the sofa.

"Rachelle?" I asked.

"Yeah?"

"You going out?"

"Yeah."

"You're going to meet Anthony, aren't you?"

"Yes, I am."

"May I ask why?"

"Why? Of all people, how could you ask me that Leslie? Look, I'm going to do what I gotta do, that's all," Rachelle said.

I listened to the sound of the running water gushing from out of the bathroom faucet, I listened to the gurgling sounds she made as she swished mouth antiseptic around and around.

"I didn't even sleep last night," she went on to say, "I couldn't. My heart was hurting, Leslie. I mean, it was an actual physical kind of hurt. I hope that you never have to feel what I'm feeling now. It's just messed up, how somebody can get you all open for them, and then just leave with no warning whatsoever. He loves me and my kids," Rachelle mocked, "bull! Anthony used me Cuz. I let that boy practically move in with me! As long as he had a place to stay, and I was hitting him off he was fine. All of that drama, and for what? He would have done better by just telling me the

truth," Rachelle said in a somewhat lower, muffled voice.

I'd never actually seen her cry before, but I pictured her tears flowing down like the trickling
raindrops which traveled right outside of the
windowpane I gazed through. It was something I
hadn't prepared myself for. "Cuz, please stop crying, you're gonna make me start up too."

"You're right," Rachelle said in between sobs.
"No more of this. I'm going over there now to
give him the rest of his stuff. It's only taking up
space here. I'm gonna tell him what I think about
him, I'm gonna tell him to stay out of my life. He's
never welcome in here again, that's for sure."

❖

Rachelle came out of the bathroom with her nose
blown, and her eyes completely dry. Not a trace
of a fallen teardrop anywhere.

"Do I look all right? I'm not trying to go out
looking all tired."

"Yes, you look fine. Probably too fine, Cuz. You
do realize that it is raining outside, don't you?" I
joked. A futile attempt on my part to raise her
spirits. No matter what, Rachelle always went out
to look her best, dressed in a blue denim outfit. It
was a top and coordinating jeans number with
black suede fringes. Her hair was hooked into its
uniquely shaped cut, like she had just stepped
out of Magdalena's salon.

"Of course I know it's raining outside, but I'm gonna be inside of the car, remember?"

"Oh yeah," I said. "Thatta-girl, let him see what he's lost, Cuz."

"Thank you for understanding, I know that I'm doing the right thing."

"I know too," I tried to reassure her. But inside, I really wasn't sure. I wasn't sure that Anthony was worth the trouble. But if it was gonna make Rachelle feel better, then I would be here to back her up one hundred percent of the way. "Did you eat anything? Can I cook up an omelet or something for you?"

"No thanks, I'm not real hungry right now. But before I go there is something I need to tell you. I didn't mention this because I was kind of embarrassed. Let me just tell you," Rachelle said, going to sit down across from me at the table. "About two weeks after Zoie's award ceremony, I bumped into Anthony in the street. I let him give me some cock and bull story for not coming, and we ended up having sex, here. I know that's all it was for him, sex, but part of me hoped that it would bring his love back for me. Suffice it to say, it didn't. So here I am two weeks later, no call, no nothing from Anthony. I finally decided to call him at his aunt's house this morning, and he agreed to show."

"You could have told me that, Cuz. Don't worry, you're doing the right thing," I said, patting her on the back. On second thought, it was worth the trouble, and then some.

Rachelle pulled the electric blue rented car up into the empty parking space in front of Anthony's aunt's house, slippery streets and all, with every ease of the professional. She liked the feel of the car, and the control she had over it. Pity it wasn't hers. The one hundred and eighty dollar a week Mazda would have to do, because her car was a passing memory. Whatever, Rachelle thought to herself. She wasn't going to stress herself about it now. Void, canceled, no feelings, no emotion, done. Emotions caused too much shit. Just then, a tall slender figure with a baseball cap was rapping on her passenger side window, it was Anthony. She unlocked the car door to let him inside. She'd be damned if she would go out to stand in some damn rain just to say a final good-bye to him. Anthony hopped in the front seat like he'd just seen her yesterday.

"So what's this all about?" he asked, turning around to glance at the overstuffed plastic shopping bag bulging with the clothes that looked too familiar. "Oh, I get it, I'm officially getting cut off right? Is that what all of this drama is supposed to be about?"

"No! Excuse me? Drama?" Rachelle asked, clearing her throat. That was the worst word in the English language that Anthony could have used. "You want drama? Well I'm sorry to disappoint you, but I simply don't have it in me anymore. Now had you been around those times recently when I needed you, you would have gotten some real drama. All the passion, emotion, tears and sweat you could have ever needed. Unfortunately, you were nowhere to be found. I haven't seen you in over a month. Do you mean to tell me that I wasn't even worth a phone call to you?" Rachelle asked, turning the key inside of the ignition, starting up the car. "Since you didn't care, then neither do I. So you can just get your stuff and get out of my car. Oh, and Anthony? I just wanted to say thank you for showing me what your definition of love is. You know, you helping me to believe in it and all. I couldn't let you leave before telling you that."

The rain was coming down even harder, but she didn't care. She wished for thunder and lightning, a tornado, a whirlwind even. Anything to take this man from out of her sight. From the distance and through rain-dropped glass, she could see Anthony's lanky body hasten across the street, with the plastic bag held high above his head. Punk, Rachelle thought to herself, he hadn't even bothered to try and explain the mess he had helped to make of her life. She'd take the blame for the rest. Rachelle shifted the car into gear and drove off down the street. At least she had done what she set out to do. She had gotten Anthony out of her life, for good this time.

"So did you do it?"

"Yes, I did it," Rachelle answered, holding the two paper bags full of groceries in front of her, simultaneously kicking the kitchen door quietly behind herself. I should have known, the look of accomplishment glimmered in her eyes.

"Where are the kids?"

"Watching a videotape," I said, helping to free her arms of one of the bags. "So what did you tell him?"

"The truth. I told him that I think we both made some mistakes in the relationship, that I tried to rectify mine, but that he never made any attempts to fix his own. That's where he went wrong. The failure of our relationship had nothing to do with the age difference. It wasn't even about the money in the end. I know that it's not completely Anthony's fault. I did stray in the beginning, but I'm wondering what would have happened had the situation been reversed. Anthony and I would still be together, no doubt."

"So now what?" I asked Rachelle.

"Now I start taking other factors in my life into consideration."

"I hope this doesn't mean that you're going to turn into some bitter-scorned man-hater or anything."

"No girl, I still love men, it just means that I'll take things slower the next time around. I'm in no hurry to rush into another relationship with any-one," Rachelle said, taking the groceries from inside of the bag and packing them away. "You know, my job is introducing a new program for employees interested in going into any specific area of health. So since I've always been inter-ested in the body and the way it works, I'm going to try and be that x-ray technician I've always wanted to be. They start out making 35K a year, girl."

"Wha-aat," I exclaimed.

"Yes they do, and my job would cover all of the college expenses."

"That sounds good, go for it Cuz!"

"Most definitely, believe me I am."

"Any regrets about breaking up?"

"Well, he was real good in bed! I might have to call him every once in a while to hit me off!"

"Cuz!"

"Cuz!" Rachelle repeated, "well I might!"

"Do you think you can really do that? I mean, just keep it purely physical?"

"Hell yes," Rachelle said, with a slow Sistagirl bob of the head. "He did it."

"Men are different though."

"See, that's where you're wrong, Leslie, women are doing it too. Especially nowadays, Look at my relationship with Anthony, that's a prime example right there. There I was, putting my everything into the physical with him, and looking outside to other men for the financial. Trust who and commitment what? That went out the window, right along with the relationship," Rachelle said with a sigh, going into the refrigerator and taking out the ground beef for lunch.

"You know, I finally broke down and told Benjamin that I was a virgin."

"Stop! No you didn't!" Rachelle exclaimed, slamming the refrigerator door closed.

"I don't know why I did girl, all he could do was go on and on about how wonderful it was that I had saved myself."

"He got a real kick out of it, huh?" She chuckled.

"Yes, just like you are!"

"No, I do think that it's wonderful that you waited for the right guy. I know it must be some ego trip for Benjamin. You should be flattered. Him going on and on about how wonderful it is simply goes to prove the point. What did you expect him to do Leslie?"

I sighed, and forced a smile. Cuz was right, what did I expect for him to do, break down and cry? A real live virgin in this day and age? Shit. I'm not even one of those women gone celibate, who's actually had sex and a messed up experience with a man. **I'm a brand spankin' new virgin**.

"So what are you waiting for, when you gonna give him some?"

"I don't know!" I blurted out. "Telling him doesn't mean the main event will happen any sooner Rachelle," I said, shaping the now sea-soned ground beef into perfectly formed ham-burger shapes.

"Oh, doesn't it?" Rachelle said, smirking and picking up the telephone receiver. "Hello Information, can I have the telephone listing for City College?"

I stepped inside of my building and walked over to the mailboxes to get out the day's mail. New York Telephone, the latest Essence subscription, and a letter from the Housing Preservation and Development, a.k.a., the director of the TIL Program.

"What now?" I said aloud, ripping the letter open then and there only to read that my building was being put on probation for not adhering to the conditions of the program. They're right, I thought to myself. I was surprised that it hadn't happened a long time ago. In fact, I couldn't remember the last time we held a Tenants Association meeting. The rent roll was decreasing, and our overall building expenses was increasing, taking a real toll on the Tenants Association bank account. Probation meant that they were threatening to let the building go back to the city, or Central Management. I trudged up the five flights of stairs and went inside the bathroom to run a nice hot bubble bath when the phone rang.

"Hey you!"

I'd recognize that voice anywhere. It was Benjamin, calling me long distance from Atlanta. "How are you, and how's your trip going?" I asked.

"It's okay, I still can't get over what you told me. I can't seem to stop thinking about it."

"Yeah, I bet you can't."

"No, I mean that I would have never guessed that it was that in a million years."

"Isn't there something else you should be doing? Shouldn't you be sailing on a boat, or taking some photographs of something right about now?"

"Maybe, but I'm not in the mood. Did I catch you at a bad time?"

"Kind of," I said, standing up to step out of my blue jeans. "I'm getting ready to take a bath."

"Then I can call you later?"

"Fine, you do that. Talk to you."

I immersed myself into the full tub of body oils, bubbles, and bathwater with the delicate scent of fresh jasmine permeating the entire room, making me grateful for the gift of my God-given sense of smell. I began sponging myself down with my new loofah. I wondered if I had made the right decision telling Benjamin about my virginity. His amusement had been just what I expected. It felt embarrassing, really. At the same time, I felt a sense of relief, as though some kind of load had been lifted, making the possibilities seemingly endless. For a split second, I closed my eyes and envisioned myself as a non-virgin. I lay back in the tub and thought real hard. Would I look different? Would I walk or talk any differently? Or just maybe I'd discover that I loved sex so much that I'd have to have it all the time. That's it, I'd be a morning, noon, and night nympho. What was I thinking so hard for? Soon I would really know. A little bird had whispered in my ear and told me so.

❖

"Come downstairs!" Benjamin said to me on the phone.

"Where are you? You sound so loud!"

"I'm closer than you think, just come down."

"Okay, okay, I'm on my way," I said, taking one last giant bite out of my turkey-bacon, on rye. I went down the stairs taking two steps at a time, my heart pounding a mile a minute. I wasn't sure if it was the stair jumping, or the angst of my anticipation. Nevertheless, I found myself standing outside in my coat, blue jeans and a gray Syracuse sweatshirt with my nightgown tucked in underneath. I stepped down from my front stoop to look up the block only to see my Boo heading straight for me with his arms open wide.

"Mmph, I missed you."

"Me too," I said. "But what are you doing back so soon? I thought that your flight wasn't due back until Friday."

"Couldn't wait until then. I had to get back to you."

"And why was that?" I asked pulling the ends of my coat together. The early morning air was nippy. "Your premature arrival wouldn't have anything to do with that little bomb that I just dropped on you, now would it?"

"A little bit?" he said. "I told you that I couldn't stop thinking about it."

"So that's what made you rush away from your vacation and your family? What is it that you want to hear me say? Or should I say, do?"

"Very funny, Leslie. All I want is for you to keep on loving me. I'm not expecting anything."

"Now more than ever, huh?" I said sarcastically. "Fine with me. If you wanted to come back early just to stare me in my face and tell me how you couldn't stop thinking about what I told you, fine. It's cold out here. Are you coming upstairs or what?"

"I wish I could, but those guys went nuts after I left. They're just like little kids needing constant supervision all the time. Why don't we do dinner? Say, nine o'clock? I'll cook," Benjamin said, giving me one last hug and a kiss.

I went back upstairs and into my bed to snuggle under the warmth of my comforter. Not the best substitute for my baby, but it would have to do.

to be or not to be

oney, where's the butter?" Benjamin asked me over the sound of clanking pots and running water from inside the kitchen.

"Middle shelf, right-hand side of the refrigerator," I answered back.

"Okay, got it!"

"What are you making in there anyway? Do I smell something burning?"

"No, you do not smell anything burning. I know what I'm doing in here you know. I'm no stranger to the kitchen. And as for what I'm making, you'll just have to wait and see," Benjamin said.

"Well how much longer do I have to wait? I'm starving in here!"

"Five minutes, Leslie. Do you think you can wait that long?"

"I don't seem to have a choice in the matter, so I guess that I can." Well, at least whatever he was making in there was starting to smelled appetizing. I was starting to get a little scared.

Good best described the delicious dinner that Benjamin had prepared. Southern pan fried steak with onions, corn on the cob, and baked potatoes with fresh sour cream.

"Well was it worth the wait?"

"Honey, you can cook for me anytime!" I said, as I savored my last bite of steak.

"Yeah, you don't have anything to say now do you?" Benjamin joked.

"No I don't," I said, planting a firm kiss on his freshly buttered lips and getting up to clear the dinner dishes from the table. By the time I had returned to the livingroom, Benjamin had laid himself out spread eagle on the rug with every light out except for the kitchen that I had just come out of.

"Why are you down there on the floor? Why don't you go and lie down on the couch?" I asked Benjamin.

"Because it's better for my back. Why don't you grab a pillow, and come down here and join me?"

"That's an idea. So, is this when you make your move?" I asked, grabbing a pillow off the couch and lying myself down beside him on the floor.

"What move?"

"You know, the move that you intend on making. . . ."

"Leslie, is this about your virginity? Because if it is, I'm here to tell you that you're way off point. I do want to be closer to you but I'm not scheming or trying to rush you into doing anything that you're not ready to do, you should know that by now."

"I know Benjamin, I know." He had taken me the wrong way. Part of me wanted him to make a move, but I wasn't gonna initiate it. Nice girls just didn't do things like that. And despite the whole situation, my mother had raised a nice girl.

"Cuz, I did it."

"You did? Oh I'm so happy for you, congratulations! What did you do?"

"I registered for school silly! You are now officially speaking to the newest member of the student body at the City University of New York!"

"Alright!. Go Rachelle! When did you do it?"

"A couple of days ago after I called the college and got the forms completed from my job. I'm just going part-time since I'm still working."

"So what classes are you taking?"

"Well for starters, I have to take a remedial math course. Girl, it's been so long since I've had to worry about fractions and percentages! Math has never been my forte. I'm also taking Introduction to Anatomy 101. I'm in school on Tuesdays and on Thursdays after work."

"That's good," I said. "The math will come in handy for practice before the kids have to come to you. So your mom's going to look after the kids?"

"Girrl-yes," Rachelle replied. "She's been totally supportive about the whole thing, which has taken me totally by surprise."

"Why would you say that?" I asked Rachelle.

"Because she never was supportive of me before. All she ever did was put me down."

"Well I guess this just goes to show you that people do change."

"I guess so, believe me I'm not complaining. I probably should be in church counting my blessings," Rachelle said.

"Church?"

"Yes church. You know that place where people go to pray, hear sermons, and get baptized?"

"Ha, ha, ha. I know, I know. I just never expected to hear you talking about church."

"Really?" Rachelle asked me. "You'd be amazed. I pray a lot," she went on to add. "I've even started to read my bible. It's a good thing. You really should try it sometime."

"I just might do that," I said. If I could find it. Lord probably only knows.

"So, Benjamin's back in town, huh?" Rachelle asked.

"Yes, he was over at my house yesterday. He made dinner."

"Can he burn?"

"Girl, he can burn!"

"So did you give him any?"

"Will you stop asking me that! For the final time no!"

"Well what are you waiting for girlfriend? I mean, what was the sense in telling him you were a virgin in the first place?"

"I told him because I thought he should know, Rachelle. He would have found out sooner or later. I mean it gets to the point where we get intimate, and then I stop him. Right in the middle of it."

"Why?"

"Why? Because I'm not ready that's why."

"Bmmph! Wrong answer!" Rachelle sounded. "It's because you're afraid, Leslie. Now what you need to do is just relax and let nature take its course! Don't you get horny girl?"

"Rachelle!"

"Leslie! Well, don't you?"

"Sometimes, . . . yes. Okay! Is that what you want to hear? Sometimes I get horny! Look, when it's time I'll know and after it happens believe me I'll be there for you to fill in all the details. Promise."

"Alright now," Rachelle replied, "I'm not getting any, so it only seems natural that you should be. I can live vicariously through your stories to get me through my little crisis."

"Is it all that bad Rachelle? Learning to live without a man, I mean?"

"To tell you the truth, Cuz, sometimes yes, and sometimes no. I'm so used to having a man in my life. There's always been my husband or somebody there. It's alright though. At least I can stretch out in the middle of my bed and not have to worry about sharing the space. Move over, stop snoring, and all of that mess. Leslie, I have more control over me, and no one else to blame but myself if something goes wrong. But on the other hand, I did like having someone to share the responsibilities of paying the bills, and taking care of the kids. I liked being sexually active instead of not looking forward to being sexually frustrated. This celibacy thing is no joke when you're not used to it. I don't know," Rachelle sighed. "I'll get through this, I'm sure."

"So how are the kids handling you and your new-found freedom?" I asked Rachelle.

"You know, it's funny, kids are much smarter than we give them credit for. They don't even ask me about Anthony. It's like they know what went down or something. I'm just glad that he doesn't work in my building anymore."

"Oh, he doesn't?"

"No girl, last I heard he was going off to join the army. Personally, I couldn't be happier for him. Let him be all that he can be."

"Cuz, you're crazy!"

"No, I'm serious! I don't wish any bad luck on Anthony. As a matter of fact, I'm still very good friends with his mother and younger sister."

"How very mature of you, Cuz."

"Don't patronize me Leslie!"

"I'm not, really. I just think you're handling this situation extremely well, that's all." I guess I thought she'd run off screaming into the night or start to stress herself so much that her hair would fall out in boxed patches. In other words, I'd underestimated the strength that had been with her all along.

"Anyway," Rachelle went on to say, changing the subject. "What are you doing today?"

"I'm supposed to be meeting up with my friend Mike. The Black Filmmaker Foundation is having a production class thing going on about location managers."

"What's that?" Rachelle asked.

"What, a location manager? Just like the name says, it's someone who manages a location. It's people in charge of finding places to shoot a film or video."

"Hmm, sounds interesting enough. Is that what you're aspiring to be?"

"I don't know. There's so many things a person can do in the field of communications. That's why I just want to try everything."

"I hear you," Rachelle said.

"So you're going by yourself?"

"Rachelle, where were you five minutes ago when I said that I was going with my friend Mike? Mike, as in the guy I met at my College Video Club meeting. We've been partners in video ever since. You've got to meet him, he is so crazy! By the way, what time is it, Cuz?"

"Leslie, you know that I never know what time it is. Wait, hold on. . . . It's 1:20," Rachelle said as she moved a bunch of books aside, pulling out her alarm clock.

"Oh my goodness! I've got exactly 45 minutes to haul my butt on down to Greenwich village for this class. We've been on the phone for an hour!" I said, dashing to my closet rummaging through to find something to wear.

"So what else is new?" Rachelle asked. "I'll talk to you later, and I hope that you have a very productive Production class."

"And if I don't speak to you, then I hope that you have a very good anatomy class," I added.

"Thanks Leslie, I will—Bye."

❖

"Yo! Where were you?" Mike asked me as I grabbed the seat he had saved for me in the over-crowded room. People were sitting on top of the horizontal tables and along the sides of all four walls.

"Couldn't they have gotten a larger room?" I turned to ask Mike.

"Leslie, what do you expect for free at NYU?"

"True, true, right, right," I joked back at him.

Just then a short stout brother with round tortoise shell specs and faded blue jeans with a hole in one knee, and a tee-shirt that read **ABOVE ALL MEANS** in heavy purple lettering entered the room.

Above All Means was a new top grossing controversial flick at the box office. My guess was that he was the location manager for the film.

"Good afternoon," he said in a deep throaty voice. "My name is Troy Wills. It's spelled just like it sounds," and he wrote on the single green chalk board: **TROY WILLS**. "I've been a Location Manager, or a Location Scout as some people might call it, for the past 13 years. I've worked on such films as *Death By An Angel*, *Firefighter*, and my most current release as most of you can see, *Above All Means*," he said, pointing to his tee-shirt.

"Thirteen years in the business? Money could have gotten a larger tee-shirt for all that time. The one he has on is a bit tight, wouldn't you say Leslie?" Mike whispered over to me.

"Shhh!" I giggled. I had no choice but to nod in agreement. The shirt was quite snug, especially right in and around the stomach area.

Mike always had something to say. It was just a part of his persona. It was just one of the reasons why I liked him so much. He knew how to keep me laughing, even when I didn't want to.

After the 40-minute lecture and ten-minute slide show, Troy handed down our first and only Location Assignment. We had to get a 35mm camera, find a supermarket, and shoot photographs from different angles as if we were showing it to a real film or video director. Not an easy task, as Troy was a perfectionist and he wanted all surrounding shots at only the most death-defying angles.

Troy wound up his lecture by adding, "And Above All Means, be totally professional."

"So do you have a 35mm camera?" I asked Mike as we walked out of NYU towards the subway station.

"No, but my brother has a real nice one. It zooms, it auto focuses, it practically operates itself. I might not even have to show up except to load the film into it. I'll see if he'll lend it to me. I'll probably have to make some kind of trade off with him. Come to think of it, he has been eyeing that Shabazz Brothers shirt I just bought not too long ago. What about you?"

"Yeah, I have one, only used it once. My mother gave it to me for my twentieth birthday."

"Yo! I hope people don't try to attack me thinking I'm up to something when I take pictures for this project. Somebody might think it's for pornos or something."

"You are so silly!" I said staring in amazement. "And you had better stop calling me yo! That's the second time today."

"Oh, I'm sorry lady Leslie, I mean yo, I mean yo-lady Leslie!"

I turned to Mike and made one of the most twisted faces I could imagine.

"Nice, nice. I like you better that way!" he joked. "So L-Leslie," Mike said emphasizing the L, "how's the old man?"

"Who are you talking about?" I asked, attempting to ignore him, scanning the passing boutique windows. "My father?"

"No, you know who I'm talking about, your boyfriend. What's his name again? Bentley?"

"No, it's Benjamin, and why do you keep calling him that? The old man! He's only ten years my senior Mike, he's not all that old!"

"Aha! So you do agree that he's old!"

"No I don't, but he is older than I am."

"Leslie, you were in Pampers by the time he entered college."

"So? Might I remind you, that was a very long time ago. I'm now 21, legal, and all woman!" I said in confident tone.

"So how's the sex?"

"Mike!"

"What? I'm sayin, he is your man. I know you're sleeping with him. How does money hold up?"

"You know Mike, I don't think I like the direction this conversation is going in. You're putting me in a position where I feel I have to defend myself."

"No I'm not, you're just being defensive! All I did was ask a question!" If this boy only knew that I was a virgin, I thought to myself.

"I'll just put it like this, I'm very satisfied in my relationship with him."

"So chief has it going on like that huh?"

"Yes he does, he's got it going on like that." I hoped he did, because the truth is that I didn't really know. The foreplay was all that. At least I wasn't making myself out to be a liar.

We started downstairs halfway on our way into the train station when Mike hollered out, "That's my train!" He leaped down the stairs three at a time, disappearing into the crowd.

"I'll call you!"

"Alright, good-bye Crooklyn!" I yelled back, as we departed on our separate ways. My destination being Manhattan, and his being Brooklyn. Now what supermarket in my neighborhood would I want to photograph?

school daze

am passing out a syllabus for the semester. It includes a brief course description, a breakdown in percentages of classwork, participation, homework, and examinations. The name of the book is listed, as well as any recommended readings that I felt would be helpful to you throughout the term. I am also passing out copies of your final research paper assignment, which will be due on the 23rd of May. There will be absolutely no exceptions unless you are ill, or in cases of extreme emergency."

Oh great, Rachelle thought to herself as she passed back the pile of syllabuses. A by-the-book receding hairline, hard to understand, unattractive professor with a speech impediment. Just what she needed, Professor Stanley Titus. Nevertheless, Rachelle knew that she had to do well, and that it didn't matter how this man sounded or looked, or how difficult any assignment seemed to be. She had to excel. This would be her chance to shine and follow her dream. She just couldn't take much more of the damn office cleaning.

"Excuse me, Professor Titus, the syllabus doesn't include the price of the textbook. Can you tell me how much it costs?"

"I don't know Miss Rhodes, but it shouldn't be over $40. Maybe you can get a used one, they are usually less expensive."

"Thank you Professor Titus," Rachelle answered. She was sure she had scored some points with him. He now knew who she was. Now all she had to do was do well in the class.

❖

Thirty dollars. Thirty dollars wasn't all that bad for the price of a used Anatomy text book. Certainly was a big sucker, Rachelle thought as she flipped through its pages. It was filled with color transparencies on color transparencies. Rachelle thought about how much she would know about the human body by the time she finished reading it. Her first responsibility had been to complete a reading of the first four chapters and to answer the questions at the end. In all, there were 28 questions. Her mother had offered to keep the kids overnight, so she didn't have to worry about them. No distractions. Now. Focus, focus. . . . focus. She sat with her chair pulled in close at the kitchen table gazing intensely at the tiny print that made up the beginning of chapter one. . . . Focus.

❖

"Rhodes, I need a clean-up on the third floor," her supervisor said as he approached Rachelle, not even bothering to look up from his clipboard.

"I know, this is the second time I've heard," Rachelle responded, tightening her grip around the mop handle she was holding. If she held it any looser, it might have just accidentally swung up and hit him.

"Then I suggest you get right on it," her supervisor answered, walking down the hall.

"Jerri-curled old knock-kneed fool," Rachelle mumbled under her breath. "Lord just give me the strength, it won't be much longer, hang in there it won't be much longer." Rachelle said those words loud and clear. She wanted the entire building to hear, and after she'd made it, she'd yell it out the window, and on top of every mountain.

hot off the grill

It's amazing how fast the time flies by. I could hardly believe that it was Labor Day, and that I had spent the bulk of the entire night before packing away my summer clothes and now taking down the fall. My sole inspiration was the search for my two-piece long-sleeved khaki linen pantsuit. It could only be the best for Patrice's bar-be-que. I was allowing Benjamin to accompany me, which honestly had me feeling just a bit apprehensive. Him being around my friends and around my crowd, was a first.

Patrice lives in her own condo, a duplex which has an exceptionally large terrace, at almost twice the size of my livingroom. Well, I've located my suit and it just might be that I'll make it to something on time for once. After bathing, dressing, and doing my hair up, Benjamin was beeping his horn for me to come down. Here goes nothing, I thought on my way down to the car. Nothing bad I hoped.

"Bar-be-que, welcome everyone, come on in now!" Patrice shouted, as we walked through the entrance of her front door. She was clad in all American colors, a red bustier, a blue denim shirt, knotted in the waist, white jeans, and red mule shoes. Wrapped around her head she wore an American flag bandanna from which her long reddish brown blunt hair stuck out on the sides.

"So, you must be Benjamin. Step all the way in here!" Patrice said, as she reached out to pat Benjamin on his back. We walked in past the foyer, where the cool hip-hop remix of Mary J. Blige was jumping off in the background.

"Patrice, don't you embarrass me," I leaned in and whispered in her ear.

"Girl please! I'm just trying to get to know Benjamin. I mean I've hardly heard anything about him, and you've been together for a while." We walked inside of Patrice's plush contemporary livingroom done up in all off-white furniture, carpeting, and cactus plants. There were cactus plants practically everywhere. I mean like every corner your eye could vividly focus in on. Why the hell she needed so many of them was beyond me. Patrice has excellent taste though, I'd never be one to knock her for that.

"Everyone, if you don't already know, this is my good friend Leslie, and her boyfriend Benjamin."

Boyfriend. Gee, I thought to myself. It sounded so foreign to have had that word associated with my name. Foreign, but good.

"Have a seat you two," Patrice said, grabbing a bar stool for herself and looking down on us as we sat below on the couch adjacent. "So, Benjamin, I hear you're into contracting. Business must be fantastic with all of the renovations going on in Harlem now."

"Well yes, I've been lucky enough to keep myself busy."

"Too busy, Patrice, this man is a workaholic," I added.

"I'm trying," Benjamin said to me.

"He's trying Leslie, you don't ever knock a man down for trying. . . . You two look real good together. I hope that you'll give me a reason to help plan a wedding." I turned around and gave Patrice one of my you-didn't-have-to-go-there looks. "One day, no rush," Patrice said trying to clean it up.

"You never know," Benjamin said. "I've tried that marriage thing, and it didn't work out. I wasn't ready, next time around I want to be sure."

"That's alright, but don't let a good thing pass

you by either. Believe me, Leslie's one of the best in the bunch."

"I know it, and I love her for the person that she is," he said.

He loves me? A public display of emotion. I moved in closer and snuggled next to Benjamin, cuffing my arm inside of his.

"Well, I see everything is under control here. You two are gonna be just fine, so I guess I should finish playing hostess to the rest of my guests. There's plenty of food and drinks. It's all set up out on the terrace. Pina Colada, Kahlua, blue Hawaii, scotch, you name it I've got it. Lance is the chef."

"Lance?" I asked. His name wasn't familiar, but with Patrice one never could tell.

"You know Lance, the chef. The one I told you about that works in the soul food restaurant in the village," Patrice said, giving me a wink.

"Oh yes, Lance, oh-kay." I didn't know who she meant, but leave it up to Patrice to find a real chef to be the cook at her bar-be-que shindig.

"Your friend is something else," Benjamin said to me as Patrice jutted off.

"Is she usually that . . ."

"Outgoing?" I said, finishing Benjamin's sentence, probably for lack of a better word on his part. "Usually, but she really is good people."

"Get your groove on! Get your swerve on!" The couples started to chant out. A few people were pairing up to dance. I only gulped down my fruit

punch, keeping both eyes aimed straight down at
the reddish-yellow pineapple chunk that had
sunk to the bottom of my cup. I didn't want to
make Benjamin feel uncomfortable because I
wasn't real sure if he liked to dance to my kind of
music and I know Patrice wasn't about to throw
on no opera. Jazz maybe, but no opera.

"Do you wanna dance?" Benjamin asked.

"No thanks," I said lying. I was only swinging
my head off and tapping my feet to every beat in
the song. Now what would give him that im-
pression?

"Come on," Benjamin said, pulling me up from
the couch. He led me straight to the middle of
the room and started to freak me, his arms and
legs moving rhythmically to the left and right,
back and fourth not missing a beat. The man
could jam!

"Let's get something to eat," I yelled over the
music, finally pulling him off the dance floor. It
had been the perfect excuse to stop dancing. He
had worn me out. We walked over to the buffet
table and piled our plates high with the tender
pieces of bar-be-que chicken, grilled shrimp, and
baby-back ribs. Potato salad, corn on the cob, and
flaky warm buttered rolls set off the meal.
"Mmph! this is good!" I said, smacking my
mouth on the end of a shrimp. Benjamin wasn't
trying to say too much on account of the fact that
his plate was damn near empty.

Someone set up a game of Pictionary and we

played that for a while. Then there was Charades and Nintendo. Patrice's bar-be-que had been a success and Benjamin and I had been accepted as a couple, an even bigger success in my book.

Who would be trying to ring my phone off the hook at this hour? I thought as I rolled over in my bed to pick up the receiver. "Hello," I answered groggily, afraid to breathe in the unpleasant smell of my own morning breath.

"Wake up call! Good morning!"

"Do you have to sound so peppy this early in the morning?" I asked glancing over at the digital clock on my nightstand.

"Girl, I got a reason to be peppy and you do too! That man of yours is a winner! And handsome! He looks like the real rugged type. How old did you say he was again?"

"35, Patrice."

"Mmph."

"Do you think I can maybe call you back after I've brushed my teeth?"

"He looks about that," Patrice went on to say, totally ignoring my attempt to get off the line. "You two look good together, too."

"Thank you Patrice," I answered sarcastically, "your approval means everything to me." Right. Why was she putting me through this form of telephone torture? I thought to myself.

"So has he started spending nights yet? No, better than that, have you given him some yet?"

"You are just as bad as my cousin Rachelle, Patrice."

"Well inquiring minds do want to know!"

"Not like it's really any of your business or anything, but no we haven't, and yes he has," I said as I propped both of my legs up onto my bed.

"You mean to tell me that you two have slept together in the same bed and done absolutely nothing?"

"I didn't say absolutely nothing, but we haven't gone all the way. Benjamin respects me too much for that Patrice."

"Hold on tight girlfriend, his own business and respectful? You better try and reel that one in!"

"Patrice, I'm going back to bed!" Then I hear this muffled gasp on the other line.

"Is he there now?" Patrice whispered, as if he would not have known who or what I was talking about before this.

"Good-bye Patrice, are you hearing me? I am hanging up the phone now." Click. That damn Patrice, I thought to myself, grabbing my pillow and turning back over to shut my eyes. She never quits. No, he's not here now. But I've got a strong feeling that if he could be, he would.

picture perfect

Rachelle couldn't help but keep looking at the paper that she held in her hand. It was the first exam Professor Titus had given and she had managed to score an A. Seems all of those late night hours of studying had paid off. Math was going almost as well. She'd scored a B– on that test. Hard work and determination could make a person do anything if they set their minds to it. "One small step for man, one giant leap for me," Rachelle said, smiling aloud to herself.

"Mommy, why are you talking to yourself?" little Tyreek asked, pouncing up on Rachelle's lap and staring up at his mother with bright, innocent eyes.

"It's like this," Rachelle began to explain,

"sometimes, when you're really happy or proud of something that you've done, you just tend to talk aloud to yourself."

"I'm really happy that. . . . my favorite Power Ranger is named Zack!"

"You see, now that felt good now didn't it?"

"Yes!" Tyreek said pouncing up abruptly and hugging his mother tightly around the neck.

"Tyreek, Mommy can't breathe, Tyreek!" Rachelle kidded with her son. Just then the telephone rang, and she reached over to pick up the phone.

"Hello? Excuse me, Tyreek, go play now."

"No! I don't want to go!"

"Two choices, go play, or go to bed."

"Okay, I'll take . . . Go play!" Tyreek shrieked loudly, running into the other room.

"I'm sorry, hello?"

"Hello," the voice on the other line replied.

It was Eustace. Rachelle would know that Jamaican accent anywhere. It might have been a few months since she had seen him, but she knew that voice when she heard it.

"So you don't know how to call people?"

"Yes, I know how, I've called lots of people."

"Oh I see, just not me right? What, I'm not good enough for you anymore? Did you know that me and your answering machine are on a first-name basis?"

"You should have left a message, Eustace."

"I didn't know what was really going on, you

see," he paused. "I didn't want to upset your household."

Upset her household? Since when? Yeah, Rachelle saw just fine. Coincidental how his English suddenly became all broken up when he couldn't come up with a good excuse for something.

"I've missed you, you've been on my mind a lot lately you know. You miss me?" Eustace asked her.

"Yes, I've missed our friendship very much."

"Good, I'm glad to hear that. You had me a little worried there. So tell me, what have you been doing so much of that every time I call you you're not home?"

"Basically, just trying to stay focused. I'm in school now."

"Oh yeah?"

"Yeah, and I'm still working, and trying to balance out the rest of my time being with the kids."

"So what kind of plans do you have today? I see I caught you at home."

"Well as a matter of fact, I was just about to . . ." Think, fast, Rachelle thought. *Grocery shopping, laundry, anything*. She'd known exactly what he was hinting at.

"I was thinking that I could maybe come over or something," Eustace went on to say.

"Come over?" Rachelle repeated. Eustace had never come to her apartment before. She had always been the one to have to go all out and see him. Maybe he'd changed. Maybe he was looking for more of a commitment. There had obviously been some changes in his lifestyle. Then again, maybe she was getting herself all worked up over nothing.

"How's your wife Eustace?"

"We're kind of separated right now."

"Separated? Get outta here." The words *Life Change! Life Change!* screeched in Rachelle's head like a red siren on top a patrol car.

"It's been about two months. We weren't getting along *tall*."

"Do you mean to say at, all, Eustace?" She joked. She really loved everything about his accent. It was so sexy.

"You know that's what I mean, at all. I've got somebody managing my store here, and I've been traveling back and forth to Virginia. I'm trying to open up a new store down there."

"Why Virginia?"

"It's nice there. Nice and green. You and the kids would love it out there, plenty of trees and grass."

Nice and green, trees and grass, same thing, Rachelle thought. "So why don't you move us down there?" Rachelle asked, amazed at her own indignation.

"If you're serious about it, I will."

Imagine that, Rachelle thought, me just picking up and taking off with my kids for Eustace and a taste of the country life, how picturesque.

"How about we talk about it when I come over?"

"Alright," Rachelle answered. Did she just say that? Too late now. Her thoughts had beat her good senses to the punch. Her thoughts had already sauntered off to the familiarity of Eustace's touch. A touch she hadn't had in a long time. "I'm at 245 Lexington Avenue, apartment 7J. I'll see you in an hour."

"Yeah mom, so did the kids get to their God-mother's alright? Good. Then I'll talk to you tomorrow. Yeah, I'll probably wind up turning in early. Bye Ma."

Rachelle hung up the receiver, exhaling a deep breath of air. She really didn't like lying to her mother, but her intentions were never bad. Her mother just didn't understand her. She never has, but there was no time to worry about that. Rachelle had to finish dressing. Nothing too revealing, just a pair of jeans and a tee-shirt. She put on a coat of goldbeam lipcolor, and was about to slip on her shoes when the downstairs doorbell rang. She hurried over to pick up the receiver when the doorman told her that there was a Eustace waiting downstairs to see her. Stay calm Rachelle, she thought to herself. "Fine, send him up please."

What in the world was taking him so long?

Rachelle asked herself as she waited. He was only coming up to the seventh floor. She walked over to the front door, opening it, hoping to catch Eustace before he got off the elevator, but he had beaten her to it. There he was looking as suave and as good as ever.

"Oh Eustace! You startled me! I thought you got lost."

"Hi sweetie," Eustace said, reaching out to give Rachelle a deep long kiss on the lips. He held her long and close in the hallway, backing her against the surface of her own door.

Rachelle could feel his eagerness. Already? Was it that old familiar friend? "Let's go inside," Rachelle said, glancing down her hallway at the doors that still all remained closed. She hoped that no one was looking through the peepholes at her. She wouldn't want anyone to have seen just how weak and ready she had been only a few seconds before. She would have to summon up every bit of strength she had to stay cool. Those forbidden memories of wild unbridled passion . . . Don't go there, Rachelle quickly reminded herself.

"Would you like something to drink?" she asked, once they were inside.

"Some juice would be good if you have any," Eustace answered, as he looked around the roomy apartment for the first time. Rachelle was doing pretty good for herself. She had a nice setup going on. Nice private building with a doorman, not bad at all, Eustace thought.

"There's no juice. I've got spring water, milk, and a liter of Pepsi."

"Pepsi's fine."

"So Eustace, what finally made you decide to come and see me after all of this time?" Rachelle asked, as she entered the room with the two glasses which clinked with soda and ice.

"I told you I missed you. I haven't seen you in over two months. A man's got a right to see his woman."

"And so here you are. So you're telling me that your curiosity didn't have anything to do with it?"

"You know I kind of sensed that you were seeing someone. True, right?" Eustace asked, with a somewhat half-closed eyes look. It was the look he gave when he wanted something. A look Rachelle knew very well.

"I was, but things just didn't work out."

"Mmhmm," Eustace murmured.

"Mmhmm," Rachelle repeated in a sexy tone. Build it up, build it up Rachelle thought to herself. Now he'll say something like you're looking better than ever.

"You're looking better than ever, you know."

"I do? Thank you." She wanted to laugh so bad. Look at him sitting there. He's so confident, so sure he's gonna get some. He was becoming less attractive by the millisecond. Since when had he broken out with those pimples on his face? And that fuddy-duddy tri-colored hat he wore over here? Thank God he'd taken it off. It was blinding, all of those damn colors. Looking like a big old clown. Him and that same familiar face, familiar gestures, and familiar compliments crap. It's all supposed to lead up to that familiar moment.

On second thought, I don't think so, Rachelle thought to herself. After all, where did all that familiarity ever leave her but lonely?

Then Eustace stood up and asked, "Can I use your bathroom sweetie?"

"It's the first door on your left."

"Don't you go anywhere now."

"I'll try not to," Rachelle answered back. No, she wasn't going anywhere, but he would be. His whole performance was so lame, she thought as she drank down the rest of her soda. Rachelle got up to take her glass into the kitchen, and by the time she had returned, so had Eustace. Only, he was undressed sitting completely stark naked on her couch, wearing that silly closed eye look that she remembered from that last time they spent at that hotel.

"You see what you did to me?" he asked.

"You can put your clothes back on now, because there ain't nothing happening here."

"Come on Rachelle, just for a minute. I bet I can make you change your mind," he said patting the spot on the couch next to him.

"It will take more than a minute to try and make me change my mind this time around,"

Rachelle said picking up Eustace's clothes and throwing them at him. "Now get dressed, and get out!"

"It's not what you think you know."

"Oh no? Then what is it? You've been here all of fifteen minutes and you're already naked! Tell me what you had in mind Eustace. Do you want to know something? I toyed with the fact that something might happen, for old time's sake. Only it seems that I've far outgrown them. And to think, I had you pegged as a friend. You could have cared less about who I was seeing. Just as long as you kept getting yours, right Eustace?"

"Right Rachelle, you never complained before. Now you're telling me that you want something more, something different? What would it have taken for me to have gotten some tonight? A move to Virginia maybe?" Eustace asked, as he pushed body parts into pants and shirt sleeves.

"No, but it may have been a start. Any other interest on your part besides sex might have done," Rachelle said, now standing at her front door.

"So you wanna talk?" Eustace asked.

"No you didn't," Rachelle said, nodding her head in disbelief. "What I want for you to do is leave," she added, holding the door open.

"Keep in touch," Eustace said as he walked past her.

Rachelle didn't even bother to reply. She just closed the door right behind him. This time

Eustace had underestimated her, damnit. She could be just as inconspicuous as the next person.

"So how did the bar-be-que thing go?" Rachelle asked me as we both climbed up on the stairmaster. It had become part of our once-a-month regimen. Health club, every third Saturday of the month. Denise would be proud.

"It really went well," I said. "Better than I could have expected anyway. Benjamin fit in just like everyone else there."

"What, didn't you think he would?" Rachelle asked, going up and down, getting a good rhythm going.

"I just thought that he might have been uncomfortable. There were so many young people there."

"You thought he might have been uncomfortable, or was it really yourself you were concerned about being uncomfortable?"

"Me, I guess. But it turned out that I wasn't at all. But you know Patrice, she's always got something to say."

"Don't tell me, she embarrassed you?"

"No, but she tried to, Talking about a wedding and all of that."

"Go-head Patrice!" Rachelle cheered, picking up her pace on the machine.

"What are you, on a death mission or something?" I asked Rachelle.

"No, I'm on a life mission girl, I wanna live!" she said, going even faster. "I wanna look as good as I feel. You know, I'm thinking about working out a little more often. I was thinking maybe three or four times a month. I'd really like to get myself into shape," Rachelle said, in an out-of-breath-tone.

"More power to you my sister, but I'm afraid that this time you walk alone. Once a month is good enough for me."

"That's okay, I can do it. I can do anything I put my mind to," Rachelle continued on to say in a clear, even, self-assured tone. "I've moved on from Anthony, I turned down Eustace . . ."

"Wait a minute, rewind, you did what to Eustace? When did you see him, and more importantly, why didn't you call me?" I said. I had gotten off my stairmaster long before.

"I saw him yesterday, turned him down flat, Cuz. It was hard, but I did it. Turns out this celibacy thing is not as bad as I thought it would be," Rachelle said finally getting off of the machine and grabbing a towel to wrap around her neck. "Girl, I'm on a positive vibe need, I just can't describe it, but it really feels good. I feel content about every area of my life."

"How long do you figure you'll be away on your celibacy trip, Cuz?" I asked her.

"Don't know, for as long as it takes, I suppose. There's a 10:00 aerobics class beginning in five minutes. Are you coming?"

"No, you go-on ahead. I'll catch up with you later. I'm gonna hit the juice bar."

"La-zy!" Rachelle jeered.

"What do you want from me, huh? I live in a five-story walk up! I'm getting all my exercise everyday!"

"Catch you later la-zy!"

"Yeah, I'll catch you later," I said. Let's see, contentment and exercising my brains out in the damn process, I hardly got the connection.

a time to remember

"I don't think that I've ever been in the park this late before," I told Benjamin as we strolled past the row of solid red benches by the trees in the children's playground.

"Don't worry, you're with me. I won't let anything happen to you," he assured me.

Not that I needed any, it was just feeling right, being with him. He made sure of that.

"Cold?"

"A little," I answered. "This weather is changing over so quickly." Small chill bumps had begun to pop up from the base of my arm.

He wrapped his arm tightly around me, which created a feeling that immediately began to warm me from the top of my head to the tip of my toes.

"So how is school coming along?" Benjamin asked.

"Pretty good, one more semester, and I'll be out. I'm really looking forward to it because that's when I start my internship."

"Oh really? Have you thought about where you're going to intern at yet?"

"Well, I'm pushing for a major network. ABC is at the top of my list."

"You'll get it," Benjamin answered confidently.

"So how's your building coming along?" I asked him.

"Good, I've almost completely renovated the inside of the whole building, new cabinets, flooring, and plumbing. I'm looking into some other properties in Harlem now."

"You going out to be the Black Donald Trump huh?"

"No, but I'm always looking out for my best interests."

"Hmm. Your best interests, that wouldn't happen to include me now would it?"

"I think so," he joked.

"Better had," I said.

"It really is getting nippy out here, do you want to head back to the house now?" Benjamin asked.

"We probably should. Maybe we could watch a video or something."

"You got any good movies?"

Pinpointing the exact time of the main event is something I cannot do. The bright colored glare of the television set, I remember. The print of the multi-blocked navy and gray comforter spread out on the carpet, I remember. Lots of kissing, and touching, explorations unfounded, oh yes, I can remember. Benjamin had lowered himself on top of me, and I lay anxiously anticipating underneath. *Were my red lace thongs sexy enough?* What a willing student I was. Touch, touch mouth, feel. When did the clothes fall off? Chile, I can't remember. His tongue tickled and probed its way over body parts of me that made me all woman. With both eyes closed and senses heightened, I remember the feel-good feel of him. Pelvic motions pumping like parts of a production line in a machinery. There was lots of kissing, and with the slightest arch of my back, an exotic explosion that brought forth combinations of pleasure and pain. "Stop!" I cried out in the middle of his bended ear. Slower, yes slower. Now go, I recall, more, yes more, yessssss! yessss! . . . *Yes! My underwear was sexy enough.*

Benjamin and I lie still, entertwined like a freshly baked bowtie, basking in the afterglow of a newly applied glaze. Benjamin rolled over, but continued to hold me close as he showered soft kisses along my face.

"You okay?" he asked me. Benjamin lay on his side with his head resting on his elbow. He was looking into my soul again.

"I'm fine," I told him. And I was. . . . I couldn't believe that it had actually happened. It felt right. The timing felt right, and the person felt right. It had been the reason I'd waited so long. Certainly was worth that wait. I was hoping that's what he saw, looking into my soul, I mean. We laid together with our bodies completely at rest. Only the television stayed on. Where was the remote? Who cared? We were both too damn tired to go switch it off.

thou shalt not . . .

he only thing I don't remember is the exact time Benjamin left, but I do know that the sun hadn't gotten a chance to make its appearance. I didn't mind. I could hardly wait to tell Rachelle. Where in the hell was she? I'd been trying to get her for the past couple of hours, but all I was getting was that stupid answering machine of hers.

"Yes Ms. Rhodes, it's your cousin a-callin. I have some urgent news to share with you, very urgent. If you check your messages call me at home, pronto," I said, hanging up the phone and screaming into my pillow. Where could she be? My class didn't start until 2:00. I decided to put some of that extra energy into cleaning up, no sense in wasting it. I was feeling brand new.

"Hey Cuz, I got your message. I'm sorry for not calling sooner but after school I signed up for tutoring in my Anatomy class. It's not like I'm failing or anything, I just figured I'd play it safe," Rachelle said to me on the phone. "If I don't maintain a B average, I can kiss this program good-bye. Well, enough about me already, what's up? I sensed that you've got something important to tell me. Maybe it was the loud display of emotion you conveyed into my answering machine, I don't know."

"Oh it's nothing really," I said to Rachelle in a lazy tone with a heavy sigh. "I'm just feeling really, really relaxed, that's all," I answered, putting an emphasis on the word relaxed.

"So, you're really, really, relaxed. That's a good thing. . . . Is that what you called me to say, that you're relaxed?"

"Think about it Rachelle, think about what I'm saying and about some advice that you recently gave me . . ."

"You didn't."

"I did!"

"You finally gave him some? When?"

"Last night, we took a walk in the park and when we got back to my house it just sort of happened."

"So how do you feel?"

"In a word? Wonderfullysatisfied."

"Leslie, that's two words."

"Maybe, but I meant it as one."

"That's funny."

"What I just said?" I asked.

"No, this conversation. It's not giving the thrill that I thought it would."

"What?"

"The living vicariously through you since I'm not getting any kind of thrill."

"I'm sorry."

"Oh, don't be. I want to hear everything that you have to tell me about you and Benjamin. As a matter of fact, I'll kill you if you leave out one single detail."

"But if it's gonna make you feel bad, Rachelle. . . ."

"Who said that I felt bad? You're misunderstanding me. I said I'm not getting any thrills out of it myself. But now when I think about it, that would be kind of sick now, wouldn't it?" Rachelle asked laughing into the receiver. "Me getting kicks off of your sexual escapades."

"You're sure right."

"I'm not supposed to be thrilled at all, except for you. So if you asked me in a word how I felt, I would have to say that I'm absolutely thrilled."

"Are you?"

"Am I what?"

"Absolutely thrilled. I mean is there a part of

you that feels like you're missing out on something?"

"Not at all, girlfriend. I've got my kids, work, school, and most of all, I've got the man upstairs to fill in all of those missing links now."

"You mean upstairs as in apartment 11F? The white guy with the sandy blonde hair?"

"No, Cuz, I'm talking about God."

"You really are getting into this aren't you?"

"Yeah, I am. I don't know how I'm doing it, but every time I turn around I'm doing more. The kids are loving church. They just started bible school last Sunday. They're learning the Commandments now. I believe they're up to fourteen, Thou Shall Not Commit Adultery. They're definitely getting a better sense of right and wrong, and they're learning to appreciate the things around themselves more."

"Who am I talking to here, Sister Theresa?"

"No, it's still me, but I'm a stronger, wiser, better, all around Rachelle. Look, I'm not saying that I'm all holier than thou Leslie, but I am changing. I don't know how to describe it. I just feel different." Just then the beep signaling Rachelle's call waiting chimed in. "Listen Cuz, I'm gonna take this one. It's probably Pastor."

"Pastor?"

"Pastor Holmes, from the church I'm going to. He promised to go over some scriptures with me."

"Oh-kay, I'll talk to you later."

"Oh, and Cuz, I really am absolutely thrilled

for you," Rachelle added in, before hanging up and clicking over to the other line.

Bible school? Pastor? Scriptures? What was Rachelle thinking about? I thought to myself, opening the tiny can of tuna to make a sandwich. This was getting to be too much. One day she was Cuz two men one woman, and the next day she's a Saint. She's gotta just be confused. And how on earth could she be so damn so-called thrilled to hear about my newest sexual exploration with her being a new Christian? The word hypocritical comes to mind, really. I'm downright positive that things between us will change. She'll probably turn into a judgmental wuss, making it very uncomfortable for me to tell her anything going on in my life. Who told her to go getting all involved in church anyway?

I didn't look any different, I didn't speak any different, and for now at least, I was convinced that I was not a crazed nymphomaniac. There was this one thing, though, the bond. It was causing big interference with my strong natured independence. I'd felt closer to Benjamin than I'd ever felt to anyone. Could it be reliance that I was resisting? Probably for good reason. I had to stay on my toes, keep my eyes open, and watch my back. We were going to the movies, and I wasn't about to be all over him.

close to home

"So how'd you like the picture?" Benjamin asked me over the table at the restaurant.

"It was sad," I said as I poured the red hot chili sauce across the shredded chicken pieces set out before me. We were trying this new Thai restaurant my friend had suggested we go to. "I mean, how does a person just risk everything like that . . . home, family, just to end up with no one, and nothing in the end?"

"Do you hear yourself talking? Isn't that what I'm doing, Leslie?" Benjamin asked, as I handed the sauce over to him.

"Oooh, this is hot!" he said, sticking his index finger into the small round porcelain bowl, taking a taste.

"So you're risking your family and home all for me?"

"You must admit, it is an identical situation. It's kind of uncanny when you think about it. Do you think you would ever do something like this if you were in my shoes?"

"I can't really say that I would or wouldn't," I answered. "If I'm unhappy, I might. Then again, family is important. Who knows what kind of person I'd be leaving them for. Suppose it didn't work out? I'd lose everything. Benjamin, I'm just trying to be real, you asked."

"According to you then, I shouldn't be pursuing this relationship right? I'm not saying that I'm definitely leaving, but it is questionable to me. That's serious. It's having less and less to do with you all the time."

"So you would have probably left anyway, had we not met, is that what you're telling me?" Hmph, a likely story.

"I don't know Leslie, I really don't know."

"Listen, I want you to continue to pursue this relationship with me Benjamin. Don't ever think it's not what I want, but I want you to be sure about what you're doing before you do it."

"Life is not that definite, Leslie. I'm not too sure about anything lately. Sonia knows that I'm seeing someone else, and that I'm not happy. Now from there, one day at a time is all I can do."

It was that kind of plain language that made me understand, or better yet, empathize. I extended my hands over Benjamin's hands and gave a gentle squeeze.

"Listen. I'm thinking, why don't we get all of this food packed up to go and take turns feeding each other at home?" he leaned in and suggested.

"Yes, why don't we?" I answered with a smile. After all, I was hungry.

"What are you trying to do to me?" Benjamin asked, as we lay entangled in what seemed to be a game of naked twister in the bed.

"I hardly know, Benjamin. Remember that I'm new at all of this!"

"Believe me when I tell you that you're a natural."

"Thank you," I said running a hand down the smoothness of his chest. I was finding it to be one of the more sensitive parts of his body. "Benjamin?"

"Yes?" he answered.

"Tell me about your ex-wife."

"Why do you want to hear about her?" he asked, turning over on his side to face me.

"Because. I just want to know, that's all."

"What do you wanna know?"

"I wanna know . . ." I said in a cutsey voice, "do you have any regrets about the divorce?"

"Not really, as far as timing went, it was bad. But I think it would have happened sooner or later," Benjamin said sighing. A look of sadness shadowed over his face. "Our relationship was like a time bomb. But I was crushed after the divorce." He paused slightly. "When the papers came . . . I wasn't prepared for that. Those papers made everything so final."

What was the point in me asking these questions again? Oh yes, I'm being a total idiot, I thought.

"We were separated for 5 years before we actually divorced."

"Really?"

"Yup." Again, I ask, what the hell was a yup?

"So what's your relationship like now?"

"It's good, better than it's ever been. We've both changed a lot, for the better."

How wonderful, I'm thinking.

"She's the top VP for an ad agency."

"Really?" Was I being redundant?

"She's about to buy a house upstate. I'm helping her close the deal since I have a little expertise in the area."

"Really?"

"Leslie, are you okay?"

"Of course I am, why?"

"Because you seem kind of bothered. Gloria and I were married, it didn't work out, so then were divorced. Now we're just good friends, that's all. Do you think you can handle that?"

"Yup, I believe I can handle that just fine." Yup,

I was determined to handle things. So that's what yup meant.

"Well honey, I've got a job in the morning. I have to be up at 6:00 a.m. so I'm gonna get going. Wanna do a picnic on Saturday?"

"That would be nice," I said, sneaking a glance at the clock which read 12:53 a.m. "Fine," I said turning over. I was so tired that it hadn't mattered. "Put the slam lock on the door."

"What? No hug and kiss goodnight?"

I dragged myself up to the apartment door, laid a big kiss and hug on Benjamin, went to use the bathroom, and made a beeline straight back to my bed. One more day before school, great.

❖

"There are a lot of you who are doing a whole lot of talkin about those people living in those glass houses! You know who you are!"

"Amen!" the congregation shouted out.

Reverend Holmes sure could deliver a fiery sermon. He had this way of making you feel that he was preaching to you and only you. A strikingly good-looking man for his matured age of 45 with salt and pepper hair, and the most manicured nails you ever did see.

"Who amongst you are ready to become a part of the divine family of Christ? To worry and weep no more? Who amongst you is ready to have a promise fulfilled with everlasting life, love, and glory!"

"Amen!"

"Thank you Jesus!" a lady sitting in the front pew yelled out loudly. From her soft demure appearance, one would have never guessed that such an uproarious sound could have bellowed from such a petite frame.

"Then I need you to do something. It's not something for me, it's something for yourself. It's one of the most important things you can do in your lifetime! Lift your hands up so that I can see who you are!" Pastor Holmes ordered in a commanding voice. "I am here living, breathing, walking . . . ! I said walking! . . ." Pastor Holmes spun around on the pulpit raising his left leg up, and bringing it down with a powerful force beneath him.

The organist played the church organ in a melodic gospel that made the room come alive, filling the space inside of your soul throughout. It was almost as if it had been a rehearsed performance, in the way each note coincided with Pastor Holmes like that.

"I say that I am here, living, breathing, walking. . . . ! It's purpose!" the Pastor shouted out. "Can I get an Amen on that?"

"Amen!!!" the congregation shouted back with hands held up high waving in a to-and-fro motion.

"My purpose is to make you understand that

there is a reward for living within God's will! People, it just doesn't get any easier than this!"

Was Pastor Holmes looking at her? She hoped not. It was just too major a move for her to make. He knew that. So what if she was practicing celibacy, so what if she read scriptures, so what if she prayed a little longer, or gave thanks a lot more often? An overnight saint she was not. No, Rachelle decided that it would be wise for her to stay right where she was. In her seat.

last chance

Just in case you aren't all aware, the reason why we had you come down and meet with us today is because your building is in serious jeopardy," Laura Matthews said, looking over heavy black horn-rimmed glasses.

The five of us sat around the circular table inside of the small room of the cluttered TIL office. In attendance there was myself; the treasurer; Mr. Hill; the president of the Tenants Association; Rosalyn, the T.A. secretary; Laura Matthews, the head honcho for the TIL Program; and Elaine Sanders, our building coordinator. Only one person, Lionel, was missing from the group. His excuse for not showing up had not been specific, just that he had something more

important to do. I'm sure we all had more important things we could do in our own lives, but we
did all manage to make it down here.

I knew this day was coming, I knew it. All of
the chances TIL had given us to get it together
had run out. Our building would be returning
back to Central Management, where the tenants
would have absolutely no control over anything.
Back to basics. The idealistic dream of buying and
owning our own apartments, diminished.

"For the most part, I'm not seeing any kind of
interest on behalf of your Tenants Association."
She continued, "I mean, why should we put any
kind of money into developing a repair plan for
your building, which by the way totals over
$100,000, into people who couldn't care either
way whether they succeeded in the program or
not? I mean, this is utterly ridiculous," she said,
using her index finger to push her frames up on
her face. The size of her pupils had magnified
tenfold.

I shifted my eyes from her over to Mr. Hill only
to discover him taking a look at his watch. Seems
he was in a rush of some kind. Wasn't he even listening? Rosalyn was on my level, I had no
qualms with her. But as the president of the Tenants Association, the person who agreed to take
on the responsibility, why is it that he couldn't
handle his business? Mr. Radical, Mr. Fight the
Power. Don't get me wrong, I'm all for the cause,
but you can't forget about the home-front. Step

down if you can't, I even tried to tell him once. Oh no, I can handle it, he would say. You kick it off, and I'll be there to take up the slack. Well pardon me, but right about now, I had slack coming out of my ears. I wasn't going to try to cover for anyone this time around. Excuses I would make no more. I was only the treasurer.

People in my building acted like I was the Super-Manager-Rent-Collector. It was overwhelming me. Yes, I'm strong-minded, but not stupid or some superior being who's agreed to handle it all. I agreed to help. I'm not getting a real salary, it's just a small percentage of the rents collected to be divided equally amongst T.A. officers, half of whom aren't even doing what they're supposed to do. All me, me, me! And thanks to the added stresses of the building, my grades are slipping. Me running up and down trying to please everybody all of the time. My life just isn't my own. But could I say all of this now? What would be the purpose? Who else was gonna do it? The accounting work, the deposits, chair the meetings and meet with the coordinator and the contractors? Whatever happens happens, that's all. I'm sick of this aggravation, I thought to myself. It would suit me just fine if we went back to Central Management. I'm still young, I can move on, and so can Rosalyn.

"Just look at your arrears, they're outstanding!" Laura still went on to say. "We need people who are going to hold scheduled meetings so that every tenant knows what's going on! If Mrs. Such and Such has a leak in her bathroom, every tenant will know who's coming to fix it and how much it's going to cost the Tenants Association to make the repair. We need people who are willing to go to the workshops we offer so that your building can stay one step ahead of the game. May I also remind you that everyone who applies for the program does not get accepted . . ." She paused. The pause was so lengthy that I thought Laura had finished speaking. "I just don't see how you can continue . . . We really have no choice."

"Well suppose we had more meetings and started taking people to court?" Mr. Hill asked, in his last hopeful sorry old tone.

"It's not like we haven't given you the opportunity," Laura answered adamantly.

"I know, but I feel like if we just had a little more time, maybe we can try and set this thing off on the right foot. We don't want to lose this program. It's all many of us have left," he said.

Boo-hoo, I thought to myself. This wouldn't be the first time Mr. Hill had put that sympathetic routine on. The odds are ten to one, Laura ain't going for it.

"I don't know Mr. Hill," she said.

"I'm sure that if we work together, we can do anything," Mr. Hill said, rolling his copy of our pending arrears into a tube.

I wondered what he meant by "we." He probably misunderstood. Thinking me, meaning myself.

"But we've been through this before," Rosalyn said disgustedly.

I think of Rosalyn as my soft-spoken T.A. counterpart. She usually didn't say much, more a sister of action than of words. Her appearance of small neatly twisted brown dreds with shells that dangled all about, and her smooth dark chocolate skin gave her the auspicious appearance that yelled out "woman of distinction." She most definitely was not one to toy with.

"All of this talking never gets us anywhere. What I want to know is, how do we get people to do what they're supposed to do?" Rosalyn asked.

"You can start by making up a list," Elaine, our building coordinator, finally spoke up and said. "Delegate tasks, formulate a plan of action, and follow through. Most importantly, write it out so that you know who is supposed to be doing what and when. This way you have it in black and white."

"I really don't know if there's time for that," Laura interrupted. "It's all after the fact. According to the TIL guidelines your rent collection must be at 60%. As it stands, you're collecting only 45%."

"Please Miss, if we could just have a little more time," Mr. Hill pleaded.

"I'll give you thirty days and no more. No turnaround, no TIL. I'll say it again: No turnaround, no TIL. Your building will be terminated from the program immediately."

"Oh thank you," Mr. Hill answered appreciatively.

Funny how I had just sat there this entire time not even bothering to say a word. I had done all I could do. We would just see what would happen next.

✦ 26

caller you say what?

Buenos tardes!" Patrice barked out after I had opened up the front door. She was holding a large brown paper bag adorned with spots of grease. I knew what it was, Patrice's bogus Spanish accent and the bag's delectable aroma made its contents a dead giveaway. Golden rotisseried Adobo chicken, fried sweet plantains, and fluffy yellowed rice. It was the Cuchifritos Combination Special. Now don't get me wrong, I was grateful for the food, but I just wish Ms. Patrice would have found me "special" enough to have called first, before she decided to drop on by.

"Girl, I'm glad you're here! I thought you disappeared off the face of the planet, I haven't seen or heard from you since my cookout. I hope you're hungry!" Patrice said, rushing past me and bringing in a breeze of energy behind her.

"Please, come on in," I joked to myself. She was already inside the kitchen opening up piping hot containers and taking up plates of food.

"So, Benjamin's been keeping you busy, huh?"

"No, it's not all about Benjamin, Patrice. I've still got this damn building, school, and this ABC internship interview coming up. It's like three months away, but I want to be prepared."

"The television station? Girl, just don't forget me when you get famous! Maybe you can hook a sista up with a position. The social service industry is getting stale fast. I could use the change after four years."

"Tell you what, let me hook myself up first, then I'll try and look out for you."

"Fair is fair. DidIshowyoumyring?" Patrice asked. I doubt that she had even stopped to take time out for air.

"No," I said, pushing spoonfuls of the flavorful rice into my mouth, thinking, the less I said the better. Patrice dangled her hand out in a price-is-right fashion, showing off the magnificent blue topaz gemstone in its gold setting.

"Go Vanna," I said.

"Ronald got it for me. It's my birthday present."

"Patrice, newsflash, your birthday's not until December."

"I know, but he doesn't have to know that," she laughed. When I think about it, Patrice has always had a knack for getting things out of men. Jewelry, money, clothes. Just about anything was possible when it came to her. "So talk to me sista-girl, what's new with you and your new man?"

I made a small hand gesture to let Patrice know that my mouth was full, and that I was chewing. Too bad it didn't stop her from talking.

"Leslie."

"Yes. . . . ?" Here it comes. I was feeling it in my bones. I was feeling it in my bones in the same way that my mother felt the sharp pains of arthritis in her legs just before a major thunderstorm.

"I was thinking, Benjamin's 35 years old. Does he have any kids?"

"Yes, a son."

"How old?"

"13, I think."

"You think?"

"Yes, I think," I answered in a calmed tone.

"You've been seeing him for awhile now, you should know. So where does he live?"

"Starrett City," I answered, covering my mouth as I spoke.

"Mm . . . hmm."

At this point, it was so quiet that I could actually hear myself chew.

"Alone?"

Now, to tell or not to tell, I thought. I carefully weighed my options. If I didn't tell her the truth, this one lie could escalate into many more. On the other hand, if I did tell her, I'd never hear the end of it. But what could she say? They're just her words. I'm grown and this is my life. Bottom line. The food in my mouth was all gone, probably chewed way beyond the 80 times it was supposed to be chewed to ensure its proper digestion. I was free to speak.

"Patrice, Benjamin lives with another woman and his son. I didn't plan it like this, but it just happened. All I can tell you is that I'm happy right now." There. I'd said it.

"Well then that's all that matters, Leslie," Patrice said, taking a sip of the juice in her glass.

"Ohgirl, I almost forgot to tell you. My friend Lance, you remember, the chef at my bar-be-que? Well, it seems that he brought his cousin with him that day, and the cousin saw you and couldn't stop raving about you."

"What's there to talk about? He doesn't even know me."

"No, I mean that he's interested. I don't know what it was. Maybe it was the way you did your hair up that day or something. See I told you to start wearing your hair up more."

"Very funny, Patrice. So you're saying that he couldn't see that I was with someone all the while he was watching me?"

"Apparently not."

"Patrice, it is not that hard to tell. You wouldn't be trying to hook me up now would you? All I want to know is, **Why** is it. . . . that a sista is always trying to hook somebody else up when

they don't even have a hook-up for themselves?"
I said lightly. I didn't want Patrice to think that I
was being overly defensive.

"Fine, it's a dead issue as far as I'm concerned," Patrice said, taking another sip from
her cup.

"All I want is for you to respect the fact that I
am in a relationship, and that I'm happy."

"I hear you, and that's that."

"Do you mean it?"

"Would I lie to you girl?"

That's that? No that's not like Patrice to give no
input to some news of that proportion. Maybe she
realizes that it is my life and that it's my decision
to make this time around. She left here in a Speedy
Gonzales fashion, just as soon as she finished eating. That's also not like her. We always talk after
eating. I wondered if she really did have a date.
Knowing Patrice, though, she probably did. It was
probably better that I left well enough alone.

"Lesliegirl, what are you doing? Do you have
your television on? Turn to channel 11."

"Patrice I'm trying to get some sleep. I've had a
week like you wouldn't imagine," I told her as I
yawned widely into the receiver.

"C'mon girl, hurry up, I'll hold on."

"Alright, alright, if it'll get me off the phone any sooner, I'll turn to channel 11," I said, getting up out of bed and switching on the set.

No she didn't. "Jenny Jones, Patrice? You woke me out of a dead sleep for Jenny Jones?"

"No wait, girl, the show is your life story, I'm telling you!"

"Don't you have to die before you have a life story?" I asked, plopping back down onto my bed.

"Leslie, this is serious. You see that guy sitting in the middle, that's Paul? Well he's being forced to choose between Lisa and Renee, you're Renee."

"No, I'm Leslie. Look Patrice, tape the rest. I promise to watch it later," I said as I yawned for the second time.

"Girlno! Renee and Lisa were going for blows before that last commercial break. I'm telling you, this show has changed my whole outlook on things. Check this out, Paul is living with Lisa, he has been for the past four years now. And, he's been seeing Renee for the past two. He's never even spent a night with her. He did spend enough time to get her pregnant, though. Mmhmm, Renee is three months pregnant. One minute he's gonna make a decision, the next minute he's not. Renee said that he told her that he only wants to be with her, but it just came out that he slept with Lisa only three days ago."

I blew out a slow rush of air. "And you're saying all of this to say what? Patrice, I'm not about to base my life around a television talk show."

"I know this is sudden, but I wouldn't be a real friend to you if I left this one alone. If you get out now, before you sleep with him. . . ."

"Patrice I already have slept with him."

Patrice gasped. "You slept with him? You made him your first?"

"Yes," I answered. "I made him my first, and second. We did it twice that night, and it was wonderful. Where is all of this coming from? Whatever happened to the real handsome rugged catch you described Benjamin as being?"

"That was before I knew what I know. Leslie, this whole thing could blow up in your face. You see what happened to that Amy Fisher person."

"Patrice, is there the remotest possibility that he could be unhappy in that relationship he's in with her? I mean, could it be that he has financial ties, obligations, and prior commitments that he has to live up to?"

"Of course. And that's not a possibility, it's called a reality of life. But he should handle his business with her first and then look into getting into another relationship. Don't you see girl? He has no closure. What, he'll leave her to go to you, and then he'll leave you to go to who? Is that what you really want? You're asking for trouble, Leslie."

"You know," I said, holding the telephone receiver in closer to my mouth, "people are so quick to judge . . ."

"Oh so now I'm people?"

"I just don't need this," I said. "I don't need you telling me how to live my life. Patrice, you don't have a crystal ball, and even if you did, you still can't see into the future. Why don't you just live your own life? You have everything you need, brand new rings, and clothes, and a big empty condo to go home to. If that makes you happy, great. Besides," I added, "I've never once said anything about you and your casual affairs . . ."

"Casual what! Okay, I'm a let you go before you say something that we'll both regret," Patrice went on to say with an edge of stiffness in her voice. "But remember this, Leslie, as long as that man is still living with his family you'll be coming home to an empty apartment! For me it's by choice. It always has been. Can you honestly say the same? You slept with him, and you probably love him now, so ask yourself if you'll be able to choose being in a relationship with a man who has to get up and go home to his common-law wife and son!"

I slammed the receiver down so hard on its cradle that I thought I would break the phone in two. Who did she think she was? Certainly not the person I had called a friend. All up in my face with all that damn green envy. I don't need her, hmph. She'll be needing me way before I ever need her.

for better or for worse

eslie, is that really you?"

"Well of course it is," I answered, straining to pull the 80 lb. handweights in up and down movements which started at my waist and ended at my shoulders.

"Imagine seeing you here," Rachelle said.

Funny, I couldn't say that I could imagine myself being in the gym so soon before the first Saturday of the month either, but it was proving to be a great stress-buster. The thought of exercising to feel good had not even begun to enter my mind before. It was obvious that Rachelle was here to look good, it showed. She was wearing a sweatband around her head and a two-piece spandex aerobic outfit, fuschia and black. She blended in perfectly with the gym's decor. Great, she'd become a regular at the place.

"I haven't heard from you in weeks. Is everything going okay with you? I've left quite a few messages on your service. One almost every day, Miss Thing. You must be real busy," Rachelle said, taking a seat beside me on the black leather bench and automatically reaching for the 100-lb. weights.

"Why wouldn't everything be okay with me?" I was starting to feel the burn in the center of my arms. No doubt I'd be sore for the rest of the week. "I mean, just because I've finally begun to take control of my own affairs? It's nothing to worry about; believe me, I'm long overdue with doing this," I said.

"No, you're right. There's nothing wrong with that. It's just that you sound real different, kind of hostile even. Was it something that I did?"

"No," I answered. We were both lifting our behinds off. I hadn't meant for it to become a contest, but somehow in my mind it had. Rachelle dropped her weights to the floor and swung both legs over to one side of the bench to face me.

"Talk to me, Leslie. Something's wrong. I know you."

"Good, then if you know me, you know that nothing's wrong. I simply need to have some time to myself, that's all," I answered, finally putting down my weights and getting up. I was definitely a sister in need of a hot shower. "I'll call you, okay?"

"Yeah, okay. Oh, and the kids are all doing fine, in case you wanted to know," Rachelle added. "You usually ask me about them."

All I could do was nod and keep walking. I was convinced that I was doing the right thing. The less people knew about me the better. Anyway, I wasn't in no mood for no sermon.

"I am so beat," Benjamin said.

"Must not be all that beat, seems you have more than enough energy for me and some things," I told him. We had just finished one of our more intense one-on-one experiences. I was loving this whole good-lovin thing. It just seemed to get better and better all the time. "You know, maybe you wouldn't be so beat if you'd stop working so much."

"I know, I know. I'm always trying to do everything for everyone but myself all of the time. I helped Gloria with some concrete work in front of the new house she bought."

"Gloria, your ex-wife?"

"Yeah."

Of course Gloria his ex-wife, silly. Who else had I known with that name? "She got the house? That was fast." I turned over in the bed, giving Benjamin full sight of my back. Was it not enough that he had helped her to purchase the house? What the hell, was he going to do all the work in it too? No, I should stop. I'm being insecure. There's no need. That's the last thing Benjamin needed to see in me. *Insecurity. Hmph.* I turned back over and wrapped both of my arms tightly around Benjamin.

"Do you know how much I love you?"

"Not more than I love you," I answered.

"You love me? This is a first for you. I'm happy that you've finally broken down and admitted it. You never told me that before. I'm proud of you," Benjamin said, giving me a wet peck on the forehead. "But I really do love you more." Benjamin planted another one on me, but this time on my lips. I still loved the way he kissed.

"Benjamin?"

"Yes?"

"I was thinking, this day doesn't have to end here. Why don't you stay the night? The whole night."

"Do you know what time I have to be up in the morning? 5:00 a.m."

"That's even more of a reason to stay. Come on. Stay. Wouldn't you like to hold me in your arms all night?" I asked, squeezing him tighter.

"I would," he sighed. "Leslie I want to stay, and I promise you that I will. But I just can't yet," he said, holding me tighter.

"Why not?"

"It's going to happen. I just need a little time.

Why do you have to rush things? Leave it alon and it will happen," he said.

So, I left it alone. And so did he. He left me alone for that night.

"Leslie, it's Patrice."

"Hey," I answered on the other end of the telephone line. It had been a little bit over two weeks since she'd called. I can't say that I was sure what to expect.

"Girl, I refuse to let a man come between us like this. I don't care what you say. I miss having you as my friend."

"You do?"

"Are you surprised?" Patrice asked.

"The truth? Yes. I almost thought our friendship was over. I'm glad you called though. If you hadn't then I would have."

"From now on, anything you tell me about you and Benjamin is fine. And I'll leave you to decide what you want to do. After all, it is your life."

"No more hook-ups?"

"Especially no more hook-ups," Patrice said, laughing into the phone. "Oh, and you weren't missing out on anything, that cousin of Lance's turned out to be a loser anyway. He's been unemployed for over a year now, and he's still living at home with Mama, girl!"

"What!" I exclaimed.

"I'm not lying ! Lance told me himself."

"How is Lance?"

"Oh he's fine. I've been seeing him exclusively ever since the bar-be-que."

"Not you!" I screamed into the phone, turning myself upside-down on the sofa.

"Yes me! He's a good man, Leslie. He works hard, and he plays hard. That's just up my alley. It's all I've ever wanted in a man."

"Patrice, I am so happy for you!" I was happy. I must have sounded pretty stupid when I tried to sound off on Patrice about her casual affairs. Who was I? The woman always used a condom. It's her rule of thumb. And look at her now. All happy and everything. "Patrice I wish you all the best, girl, I really do."

"Thanksgirl. How's your man?"

"Alright, we're hangin in there," I said.

"Good, you swinging from chandeliers yet?"

"You think I'm not when I am?" I laughed. The light socket was more like it, but I was definitely swinging.

"Well I'm gonna let you go now. Let's get together this week. Your favorite restaurant, your treat?"

"Sure, my treat. I'll call you Thursday night."

"Alright, I'll talk to you later, then."

"Oh, Patrice?"

"Yeahgirl?"

"Thanks for calling."

"Anytime, all the time, girl."

power in prayin'

The word exhaustion could not even begin to describe the day she'd had. Rachelle wearily slipped arms that struggled to stay up through the open holes in the long flannel green and white checkerboard boxed nightgown. It gave her the sense of comfort she had been seeking all day. There was certainly no comfort to be found working a full 8-hour shift at that office building. All day it was clean up on floor two, clean up on floor nine. Felt like she'd worked eighty hours instead of eight. Then going to those two night classes that demanded she trek on the train directly after work, going past the stop that would lead to her house, leaving her off somewhere in Upper Manhattan. Her school agenda called for one micro-

review and one algebra exam, all within the con-
fines of three hours. Still, she managed to arrive
home early enough to pick the kids up from their
grandmother's. Only to bring them home, run
baths, help with nightclothes, and dramatize a
bedtime story whose characters consisted of two
tube-sock puppets. It was all so wearing. Rachelle
knelt down on her knees next to her bedside, with
hands together and fingers intertwined, and
bowed her head down.

*Lord, it's me Rachelle. I barely made it down
here to talk to you. There's a strong possibility
that I'll just yank the covers off my bed and sleep
right here where I am on the floor, as tired as I'm
feeling. But I knew that I wouldn't be able to shut
my eyes, not before giving you the praise. I just
wanted to continue to take time out to thank
you. Thank you for my children, Lord. Thank you
for Zoie, who keeps me smiling with her grown-
up antics. Talkin' about she's got a boyfriend
now. Five years old with a boyfriend! I better
never run into him at that pre-school class of
hers, I'll tell you that.*

*And that Jaree? Well he's just my little
grasshopper, that's what he is. Can't seem to keep
still for more than 30 seconds, always jumping
around somewhere. No wonder I'm always in the
shoe store, the boy can't help but wear his soles
out. And let me not even speak about Tyreek, he's
quite the little man for his age. Wanting to take
out the garbage, and screen my phone calls. I'm*

proud of him. I know he'll make some lucky young lady proud someday.

Thank you for my mother. Even though she gives me a hard time, she's always been there for me, as my anchor. Thank you for giving me a job to go to in the morning, and a college to go to at night. Thank you for the roof over my head, and the food in my home. Thank you for my cousin Leslie, Lord. Please help her to see that I'm still the same person I've always been to her. Please let everything work out between her and Benjamin. And Lord? Please help me to bring you closer to becoming a bigger part of my life. I realize that nothing is possible without you. And thal special man that you've chosen for me? Do you think you could send him along any sooner? The flesh is so, so weak. Oh, and Lord? Before I make this attempt at getting back up, I especially want to thank you for Fridays.

Amen

"Hello!"

"Hi! Who is this?" the little voice asked.

"Bmph!" the phone sounded, letting off a high automated shrill.

"Zoie! Stop pressing buttons on the telephone girl! Has it been that long? Do you mean to tell me that you don't know your big cousin's voice when you hear it?"

"Leslie! Hi! You know what? We're going to the park today!"

"Oh yeah? That's wonderful, but isn't it kind of cold outside?"

"Yes, but Mommy says that she's going to dress us real warm."

"Okay now, I wouldn't want my babies getting sick on me. Where are the others?" I asked Zoie; she was such a little woman, eight years old, going on thirty. She was so advanced in every little thing, it was far easier to mistake her for the thirty-year-old than the eight-year-old that she really was with the way she went on.

"Oh, they're getting ready."

"And where's Mommy?"

"Right here, okaybye Cousin Leslie!"

"Bye baby."

"Hello?" Rachelle said greeting me in a warm tone. "I knew you'd call, you were in my prayers you know."

"Was I Cuz? Well right now I need all the prayer I can get," I said. I was doing my best to relate. I'm sure it's complimentary to be in someone's prayers.

"Anyway, I hear you're going to the park."

"Yeah, wanna hang out with me and the kids?"

"I'll be over in a half an hour."

❖

"I guess I've been acting like a real jerk lately," I said as I lifted Jaree onto the upper level of the dome-shaped metal monkey bars.

"You're guessing right. You have been a real jerk," Rachelle answered as she held Jaree up on the opposite side of the bars.

"It's good that you agree with me and all that, but aren't you a Christian now?"

"What's that supposed to mean? Leslie, people don't change overnight. I don't know why you're making me out to be this icon of perfection. For future reference, you should know that our relationship is not going anywhere, and that I'm not here to judge you. I'll always be here for you."

"I know, but it seems so much different now."

"Why because I curse less, or because I'm not involved with anyone? Or is it because you're having sex and I'm not?"

"It's all of those things in a way," I answered, walking over to the swing to push myself off the ground with both feet held high in the air. "Rachelle, it's like, how can you talk the talk if you don't walk the walk?"

"But I have. I've been there, you and I both know that. One thing we'll never have is a problem relating to one another."

"That's true," I agreed.

"I know it is. So what's been going on with you?" Rachelle asked.

"Well, Benjamin and I are doing alright. I know that our relationship has gotten stronger. We're closer than ever I think. He just works so much. There just aren't enough hours in a day for him."

"Excuse me, Jaree! Zip that coat back up! It is not summer out here!" Rachelle yelled out to her son.

"But Mommy, I'm hot!"

"You'll be even hotter after you get sick with a temperature, and have to get rushed to the hospital. I'm pretty positive that there's a big needle with your name on it just waiting for you there!"

"No! I don't wanna go! I'll zip my jacket back up, Ma!"

Rachelle and I looked at each other and laughed.

"So what was I saying? Oh, I was about to say that it's good that things are working out. And about that work thing? You knew he was a workaholic before you met him, so don't go expecting any overnight miracles. The man does what he has to do to earn his living, Leslie."

"Just as long as he makes time for me, I won't complain."

"He is making time though, isn't he?"

"Oh yeah, but I find myself sometimes questioning if it's enough."

"It's never enough when you're in love with someone," Rachelle said.

"I know, believe me I know," I told Rachelle. I was working on those nights. My patience was starting to wear thin. It wasn't like we hadn't been together long enough. Five months was more than enough time.

"As long as you're happy, Cuz, I'm happy," Rachelle said, reaching to give me a hug.

"I am. I do love him, I really do. I've never felt this way about anyone."

"Ain't that cute, my cousin and her first love. Let's hope it's your final one, too."

"I hope so. I'm not crazy about the situation I met him in, but since I didn't plan it, I'll have to deal with whatever consequences come my way."

"That's life for you."

"Cuz, do you think everything will work out?"

"I'm sure that it will," Rachelle answered.

If Benjamin had not started spending nights over, nothing was gonna work out. Nothing at all.

flashlight

Is that your pager lighting up like the Rockefeller Center Christmas tree?" It wasn't all that difficult to notice the red blinking black box on Benjamin's hip. It was especially recognizable as we walked through the door of my darkened apartment, with all the lights inside turned off.

"It's probably those guys," Benjamin said, glancing down and pressing the small button which lit up the tiny green electronic screen. "They refuse to let me have a moment's peace."

Truthfully, it hadn't been the first time, nor would it be the last time I'd seen that pager blow up like that. If Benjamin was with me, it was sure to be vibrating, beeping, or blinking. Benjamin made himself at home, stepping out of his pants, pulling his sweatshirt off over the top of his head. "Honey, could you get me a washcloth and a towel? I want to clean up a bit."

❖

Okay, so he's cleaning up a bit. I'm here, and so are his pants. The same pants that have that pager clipped onto it. The same pager that keeps blinking with that damn red light. I casually motion myself over to the pants to press the button that reveals the number . . . 718 555-5824. Easy enough for me to commit to memory, but better to keep written down, just in case, I think to myself. I hurriedly go into the other room to jot down the number, knowing that he could walk in at any minute . . .

"That feels better," Benjamin said, dabbing his head with the towel, coming over to give me a peck on the lips.

"All done?"

"Yeah."

I wondered if Sonia could tell if he smelled any different after he got home. Maybe we used the same brand of soap.

"So what do you wanna do tonight?" Benjamin asked me.

A perfect answer would have been, I want to see how long you're gonna stay, or, I want to see just how serious you take this relationship. Instead I simply replied, "Just kickin back is fine with me. We can shoot the breeze a bit." Shoot the breeze? What was that about?

"Did I tell you my dad's coming in town on Thursday? I can't wait for you to meet him," he said as he stretched out across the couch.

"Really? Well I can't wait to meet him either. Are you anything like him?" I asked, taking a squat next to him with my legs folded on the floor.

"No, but we both work a lot," he answered with a throaty laugh.

"Figures, with your drive it must be hereditary," I said, as I played with his fingers. I'd never noticed how large and worn they were, the working-man hands with the rough look and gentle feel.

"So how's Cuz?" Benjamin asked me.

"She's good. I spent the day with her and the kids on Tuesday."

"And how's Mom?"

"Fine, she's getting herself all ready for Thanksgiving."

"Yeah? She goes all out, huh?"

"Always. I love it when she goes all out, though." Thanksgiving, our first major holiday, I thought to myself. What were the chances that we'd be spending it together?

"My brother invited me over to his place on Long Island. His wife's cooking," he said.

Was that a spot on my rug? I tried to put the focus on anything but what Benjamin had just said. The best thing I could come up with was "that sounds nice."

I could just see them now. In my mind, I pictured Benjamin, Sonia and their son, his brother and his wife, and their siblings all sitting around a long table with the big browned turkey on a silver tray. There's place settings, and a huge floral centerpiece of red roses, eucalyptus, and over-ripened yellowed squash. There's homemade cranberry sauce, and bone china, too. Everyone's smiling and happy. The only thing not there is me. But don't get me wrong, my Thanksgiving dinner is delicious. I've got a browned turkey and cranberry sauce, macaroni and cheese, greens, sweet potato pies . . . the works. The table is a little less fancy. There's no centerpiece, and we're dining off of styrofoam plates. That's so that we have less dishes to wash after dinner, I'm not planning on washing anything. It's myself, my mom, my aunt, and some cousins. Lots of cousins, really. Everyone's smiling and happy, or presumably so. The only thing not there is Benjamin. It certainly does put a new spin on the meaning of giving thanks. Thanks for . . . life. Thanks for . . . good soul food. Thanks for . . . family. Thanks for hope?

"How would you like it if we spent Thanksgiving together?" Benjamin suddenly asked me.

"How is that possible?" I asked him, taking up the remote control and flipping channels. "I mean, is she going out of town with your son or something?"

"Leslie, she knows," he said, abruptly placing both hands behind his head as he laid across the couch."

"She knows?" I asked in a surprised tone.

"We had a long talk. I told her I was unhappy."

"So? You've told her you were unhappy before. What makes this time any different?" I asked. I was smart enough to know that saying had nothing to do with doing.

"You . . . us, that's the difference."

"So she also knows that you don't plan to spend Thanksgiving with her then?"

"No, but I'll just have to tell her."

"What about your son?"

"I don't know yet. We'll see what happens, Leslie. I'm just trying to take this thing one day at a time."

"I just can't believe that she's taking this thing so lightly."

"I never said that. She's upset, but just not showing it. Part of her is hurt but she won't admit to it. She's convinced that this is just some kind of phase that I'm going through. Almost like she's saying I'll get over it."

"Well is it a phase?" I asked. I'd just put the remote down, and I'd just stopped flipping channels.

"Doesn't feel like it. I think that if it was, that I wouldn't still be here. By now, the average man would have been satisfied."

"Because we've already slept together, because

you've been my first right? Go ahead, you can say it."

"Right, Leslie, you're right. But like I said, I'm still here."

"Well, who would we spend Thanksgiving with?" I said, changing the subject. I didn't want to press him. "My mother would have a fit if I wasn't with her."

"How about we go to both places? We'll just drop by. Your mom's, my brother's. Are you ready to meet my family?" he asked me.

"I am if you are. The question is, are you ready to meet mine? At least you'll finally get to meet Rachelle. I talk about her so much, I feel like you two have already met."

"Seems like it. Honey, do you mind if I take a little nap on you? I'm bushed. I must have unloaded 1000 lbs. of cinderblocks today."

"No I don't mind, go ahead." I told him. He'd already told me everything I needed to hear.

❖

He just left. It's 7:37 a.m. That would make it an overnighter now wouldn't it? He was sleeping so hard after he dozed off. Poor guy. I even tried to wake him, around midnight. Midnight being the official beginning of the next day. I'd waited until then. After telling him what time it was, I got okay thank you honey, and a kiss on the forehead. He then proceeded to get up, I thought he was

going to leave, but instead he grabbed a comforter, and hopped back into bed. So I cut off the
TV, showered, and hopped back into bed with
him. Now it's morning and I kinda don't believe
that it wasn't just a dream.

wayward bound

ord, I don't always go the right way . . . but you're still callin' my name!" the choir wound down after singing a strong round of chorus. Pastor Holmes stood up from the large velveted burgundy colored chair, and took his place in front of the pulpit. "I'd like to welcome you all to the Holy Christian Faith Temple this morning. As I look around the church I see some faces that I haven't seen in a long time, and I see some faces that I've never seen before. Would all of the faces that I've never seen before please stand and give us your name, so that I can add you to the list of old faces that I've seen before. There are no strangers in the house of the Lord."

Pastor Holmes was something else. You could always count on him to keep it real.

"You don't have to feel committed, you don't have to feel any anxiety. Maybe you already have a church, or maybe you just dropped in to fellowship with us on this pre-Thanksgiving Sunday," Pastor Holmes said, flailing arms out of his gold robe. "Whatever the case, we're glad to have you here with us."

Three new people stood up. Two women, and a man. A medium-height coffee-colored man with a clean-shaven bald head of just the right size and contour. Lord, I hope you're not hearing what I'm thinking to myself right now, especially with me being in church and all, but I figure that I'm in the right place if I'm gonna repent about anything.

"Hello, my name is Nathaniel Wallace," the smooth-shaven gentleman said aloud to the congregation. "My aunt is Ms. Ellamae Wallace, and she invited me here this morning. I'm very glad that she did."

"Amen!" Pastor Holmes shouted out.

Ellamae Wallace was his aunt? Well what do you know, Rachelle thought to herself. Ellamae Wallace was one of the most dearest, sweetest people you could ever want to meet. Ellamae Wallace had opened arms up to me from the first moment I'd stepped inside of the church, encouraging me to become a part of their extended family.

Everyone went upstairs to eat the food that some sistas in the church had prepared at the completion of the mid-day service. The menu included smothered turkey wings, baked macaroni, steamed cabbage, and black-eyed peas and rice. Rachelle stood on the lengthy, winding line waiting to be served.

"Excuse me, is this the line for food?" a handsome Nathaniel stepped over to ask.

"Food? No, but if you want the line for the ladies room, this is the place," Rachelle joked.

"Seriously?"

"No," she laughed. He had quite a set of eyes on him. Dark. His eyelashes were long, and his eyebrows kind of arched. They were the kind any sane woman would kill for.

"Hi, I'm Rachelle," she said, extending a hand out to greet him. "And you're Nathaniel, right?"

"Yeah. It's good to meet you Rachelle."

"Where's Ms. Ellamae?" she'd asked stepping up closer to the front of the line, which had started to move.

"Oh, she's around here somewhere I'm sure. That was a good sermon that Pastor . . ."

"Holmes," Rachelle answered, helping him to complete his sentence.

"Yes, Pastor Holmes did give a damn good sermon today," he said, correcting himself.

"So, are you a regular church goer?" Rachelle asked, smoothing over her skirt.

"Not really, but I have been looking for the right church."

"That's good, I'm pretty new here myself. I've only started coming two months now."

"What'll you have Sista Rachelle?" a plump Sista Thomas asked her from behind the table armed with a heaping spoon and trays and trays of large aluminum pans set out before her.

"Everything, Sista Thomas."

"That would be the usual then!" Sista Thomas said laughing, heaping up the mounds of hot steamy food.

"And this is my friend Nathaniel, behind me," Rachelle said, turning around to smile. "Hook him up too, please,"

She hadn't waited for a reaction, or for Nathaniel to get his food. Instead, she went on to find a seat for herself in the back of the room with her plate.

"Mmmm!" Rachelle mumbled, savoring a tasty bite of tender turkey. Everything tasted so good. It should have been a sin to have eaten so well two days before Thanksgiving. She looked up from her plate, and saw the tall handsome Nathaniel looking around the room. He looked kind of lost. Rachelle scooped up a spoonful of the cheesy macaroni pie into her mouth.

She watched him as he turned his body slightly, first to the right, then to the left. His profile was picturesque. His skin, smooth and unblemished, and that bald head? Definitely trouble. She imagined skimming her tongue across it. "Forgive me Lord!" she said aloud. Why was she always going there? Why couldn't Nathaniel just be a friend? Why was her mind already trying to turn them into a couple? "Lord, please forgive me."

"Lord forgive you? Is it that bad?" Rachelle looked up to see Nathaniel standing in front of her with his plate in one hand, and a tall pink lemonade in the other.

"Don't mind me, I was just thinking out loud," Rachelle answered.

"I was looking for you. You disappeared on me," he said. He was still standing there.

"Well, you're welcome to take a seat here."

"Thank you." He placed his food on top of the table, pulled out his chair, said grace, and started eating.

A man who said grace before eating. How refreshing, Rachelle thought.

"This food is delicious," Nathaniel said in between bites.

"So did you ever find your aunt?" Rachelle asked, using her knife and fork to cut off pieces of the smothered turkey.

"Mmhmm. So where are the kids today?"

"At their grandmother's. How did you know that I had children?" Rachelle asked him.

"Because I've seen you with them before. Zoie, Jaree, and Tyreek are quite a handful you've got there," he smiled.

So he'd seen her and her children before, and he knew all their names? When did that happen? She wondered what else he knew.

"Tell me about it," Rachelle said, "but I thought this was your first time visiting the church."

"No, actually, it's my second. I just never stood up the first time." His plate was clean, as he forked up the last corner of rice.

"So you liked the service so much that you decided to come again?" Rachelle eyed the huge piece of turkeybone on her plate and wondered if Nathaniel would think ill of her if she picked it up with her fingers and savored all of its goodness into her mouth. She decided to go for it.

"Yes," he said as he smiled and took a drink from his cup. "You know, I can admire a woman with an appetite as big as mine."

Rachelle decided to take the good out of that comment. No, she wasn't afraid to be herself, that's what she took it as. She looked across at Nathaniel as he drank down his lemonade. She'd never seen anyone swallow liquid matter so fast.

"I feel like something is missing in my life. I'm 36 years old, I make a good living, but something is missing, I'm just not happy."

She hoped that he wasn't an excessive talker. She was liable to fall asleep on him, especially on a full stomach.

"You ever just felt like you wanted to do a 360-degree change in your life? It's like, you hated the things you did in the past, and you want to make up for it now?" Rachelle nodded her head yes, and continued eating.

Boy did she ever know what he was talking about. She would have spoken, if there wasn't that incessant need to hear more of what he was saying.

"Church makes me feel good. I'm not trying to get saved overnight, because I know that I'm not ready. It's a real serious commitment to make."

"You should only do it when you're ready to," Rachelle said agreeably.

"Are you saved?" he asked, seeing that she was finished with her food.

He took up both plates and got up to throw them in a garbage can that was not far from their table.

"No, I don't feel that I'm completely ready either. Sometimes I feel like I'm just making an excuse for myself. Especially when I think about all that Jesus did for me."

"That is so true," Nathaniel said. "I was just talking about that with my aunt. You know she's been saved ever since she was a little girl."

"That's not hard to believe, she's pretty dedicated."

"I think she was twelve years old. I was trying to tell her that I would like to get saved, but it wouldn't make any sense for me to do it, if I was just gonna turn around later, and go buck wild."

Had he been buck wild? Rachelle thought to herself.

"Believe me, I've been there. I'm so thankful that I got this new job."

"What do you do?" She'd bet a million to one that he'd say office worker. He was so conservative looking. The charcoal gray suit, the pastel yellow tie, and the black wing-tipped shoes.

"I'm an auto mechanic," he answered. "I've had my license for a while. I just never put it to good use. I'm in the process of opening up my own shop. I'm at the end of my apprenticeship right now."

"That's great," Rachelle said. So she'd been wrong, and?

"And what do you do?"

"I'm in office cleaning right now, but I'm going to school for radiology."

"Really? That's fascinating," Nathaniel answered.

"Which part, the office cleaning or the radiology part?"

"I'm thinking both. You're divorced right?"

"Who in the world is sitting around telling you all of my business?"

"My aunt casually mentioned it to me."

"Oh did she?"

"Yes, but don't worry, she didn't volunteer any information. It was only after I'd asked."

"You asked about me?"

"Sure did. I like the way you carry yourself. That's why it's fascinating how you're taking care of yourself and your family, and going to school to study radiology."

"Thank you," Rachelle answered. She couldn't

be angry, not at one of the sweetest, kindest, people she'd ever known.

"Would you do me the honor of going to dinner with me sometime? It's just dinner, I promise. I know that your schedule's hectic. Whenever you say is good for you, is good for me."

"I'll have to see," Rachelle told Nathaniel.

"Good enough," Nathaniel said getting up from his chair.

"You're leaving?" Rachelle asked. She hoped it wasn't because she hadn't readily accepted his dinner invitation.

"Yeah, I'm gonna try to find my aunt, and see if she wants a lift home, or if she's gonna stay here."

"She'll probably stay," Rachelle said. "Sista Ellamae is usually one of the last people to leave."

"Take care, and tell the kids I said hi," he said, as he went down the steps of the church. "See you next Sunday?"

"Yeah, I'll be here," Rachelle answered. "Oh, Nathaniel? The next time that you have any questions, come to me. Don't go to anybody else."

"I thought that was what I was doing. . . . didn't I ask you to dinner?"

thanksgivin' one

kay, so it's now 4:49, and I'm all done reminiscing. I'm dressed. It's the two-piece cotton mocha pant suit, and I've wiped my sweaty palms off, and my mind is still persisting. I'd have to call this one of those times. . . . that I want to be bothered. Damnit! It's Thanksgiving. People are waiting. And if my mother calls here just one more time, wanting to know when I'm gonna get there. . . . I know that the turkey's ready, and I know that the yams came out just right. The sauce isn't too sweet, and she's added just the right amount of lemon and nutmeg. And I know that Aunt Bertha's been asking for me cause it's the reason she drove in those 14 long miles from Baltimore. I'll be there, but not before

I scream, if my mother calls me again. Then the phone rings. But just as I'm about to open my mouth and belt out a big one, the doorbell goes off. I'm gonna have to go with the door on this one.

"Finally!" I said aloud; my razor-sharp attitude was gone. Time was no longer of importance. Seemingly, I had more of it. Benjamin had made it here, when I needed him.

"Sorry I'm late, but I had a pipe burst on me in my Astoria building. I had to get someone in there right away to make the emergency repair."

"I figured it was something along those lines," I said, looking him over. He was dressed in an off-white cable-knit sweater, with a matching turtle-neck, a pair of slacks, and some brown dress shoes. He looked pretty nice, but something wasn't right. I reached over to straighten the fold on his turtleneck, even before he could step all the way inside of the apartment.

"Do I look okay?" he asked as I struggled with the fold.

"You look great," I told him. "How do I look?" I asked, as I took a step back in front of him.

"Wonderful as usual, minus the nerves."

"Now why would I be nervous?" I said, rushing off into the livingroom to check my face.

"Honey, you look good, relax," Benjamin said, wrapping his arms around my waist from behind. We both looked good, I thought as I gazed at our reflection in the mirror. The perfect Thanksgiving couple.

Now all I had to do was be cool. Cool meant that I wouldn't be getting bent out of shape feeling all of his family's eyes upon me, watching my every mannerism, my every move. Cool meant that I'd be sociable and helpful, not isolating or unnecessarily abrasive. Cool meant knowing people are gonna talk, regardless.

"Well, I thought you two weren't going to show up!" Benjamin's brother said, as he greeted us at the door.

"You can blame that one on this one!" I answered, physically poking a finger into Benjamin's side.

"I should have known," he said. "Don't tell me, it was some kind of construction catastrophe right?"

"Right again Bro," Benjamin answered. The two exchanged a masculine hug. So this was Benjamin's brother. I noticed the resemblance, same height, nose, and confident stance.

"You must be Leslie, I'm Vernon. How in the world did this man luck up to find somebody as pretty as you? He told me you were a knockout, but my goodness!" his brother said, showing us in and taking our coats. I was ready to marry into the family after that introduction. Then the wife came in. A medium-height brown woman with Chinese features and long wavy hair down past her shoulders.

"Benjamin, you finally made it!" she said, reaching to take his arm and pull him into the den. I noticed that she peered at me. I accepted it as an acknowledgment because I'm cool like that. I could hear Benjamin's voice before Vernon and I could enter the room.

"Lisa, I want you to meet Leslie."

"How are you?" I said, stepping into the den as if on cue. Again, she peered at me, like I was there, but I wasn't there. "Anything I can help you with?" I offered. No one could tell me that I wasn't good.

"Oh, no thank you, really. I don't need you to do a thing," she replied. There was something about the tone in her voice. One look over at Benjamin's face told me all I needed to know to get me through. It said, please Leslie, please Leslie, keep your cool.

By now, I already had it all figured out. When it came to Benjamin and me and our relationship, as far as his side of the family was concerned, the men would love me, and most of the women would love to hate me.

"So where's Sonia and Kareem?" Lisa asked.

"Sonia and Kareem are where they're at, I suspect enjoying Thanksgiving dinner," Vernon said in a stern voice. He was probably used to his wife's antics.

"Uncle Benjamin!" Two kids came running into the room, one of each gender.

"Hey!" Benjamin said, lifting both children up into his arms.

"Honey, they're fraternal twins!" he told me.

"They're so cute!" I answered. "How old are they?"

"Nine!!" they both answered in unison.

"And they cost $90,000 a year to feed and clothe," Vernon said smiling.

"I'm Leslie," I said, walking over to the twins, "and what are your names?"

"Kenar and Kenya," they each answered.

"You're pretty," Kenya told me.

"Thank you. I think you're very pretty, too. Kenar, do you have anything to say?" He was just blushing all over the place.

"Where's your bathroom?" I asked Vernon. I had been holding it in long enough, ever since before we had left my apartment.

"I'll show you!" Kenar said, hurriedly getting down from Benjamin's arms and taking my hand, guiding me out of the room. The house was immaculate, just as I'd imagined it to be. Gothic olive antique furniture and beveled glass and brushed gold in every room. I hadn't imagined, however, that I'd be going past the kitchen to hear Miss Lisa on the phone.

"Sonia, I just can't believe that Benjamin could bring that woman into this house. When Vernon told me he'd invited her to come along, I never dreamed she'd actually have the audacity to show up. And she looks likes money. She must have put on the best thing she had in her closet. Don't laugh, I'm thinking about poisoning the homewrecker's food! Stop laughing Sonia, I'm serious!" she said, as she laughed along.

"Oh, is that Sonia?" I asked. "Please, tell her that I'd like to wish her a very Happy Thanksgiving," I said, walking inside of the kitchen.

"Happy Thanksgiving Aunt Sonia!" Kenar yelled out.

Busted. Twice. Lisa stood there just as embarrassed as she could be. Of course she tried to play it off, and why not? Everything in the kitchen was prepared and ready to be set out on the table with all of its homely smells meant only for the welcomed.

"Yes, did you hear that?" Lisa asked speaking into the telephone. "I'll speak to you later," she said. "You do know that you're way off here, don't you?" Lisa asked, putting the phone down gently onto its receiver and then taking up a big spoon and dispensing the green string beans into a large Corningware serving dish.

"Don't you want me to show you where the bathroom is?" Kenar asked pulling on my hand.

"No. You go back into the den with your father

and Uncle Benjamin," she hesitated. "I'll show Leslie where it is."

"Oh-kay," Kenar said, literally stomping his way out of the kitchen.

"You know what, Lisa? It really doesn't matter to me. This little game you're playing, I realize that I don't have anything to prove to you besides the fact that I'm a decent human being. And I've already done that, so if you can see your way through tolerating me in your home this Thanksgiving I promise not to stick around one second more than I have to," I said, with my head held high. I pushed the swinging kitchen door open real wide and hard, thinking it should have been Lisa's face.

❖

"Somebody sure is real quiet," Benjamin said to me as we turned into the block towards my mother's house.

So. And? I thought to myself as I stared out at the road in front of us. I'm a true believer in that old saying that if it ain't broke, don't try to fix it. I'd been quiet throughout the majority of the Thanksgiving meal, which despite the circumstances turned out to be quite tasty.

I did however, happen to write a letter on a table napkin in my purse while on my brief visit to the bathroom. It read something like this: *If I'm dead, it's because Lisa Bailey poisoned my food*. I signed and dated it, thinking that I was better off safe than sorry. I'm greedy, but I haven't lost total control of my mind yet. And can you imagine? Ms. Lisa was going all out of her way to be extra nice to me. Offering me food, showing me the house, and suggesting that we shop together sometime. That's a joke. I wondered what Sonia would think if she got a whiff of our budding new friendship. But it's okay. One might wonder if my behavior had been somewhat superficial. I'd say, most definitely.

And now that we're in the car, away from everyone, Benjamin wants me to speak? My mother's gonna kill me, that much I knew. I hadn't even tried to call. She'd never understand how I could have had Thanksgiving dinner at someone else's house and then come to hers.

thanksgivin' two

"I t's the first building on your right," I told
Benjamin as he pulled the car over into the
empty parking space. "And if my mother gives
you any attitude, don't stress it. The odds are
totally against us. We're late, and we've already
eaten. So don't look for too much of that southern
hospitality." Benjamin looked over at me and
smiled, arching his eyebrows up in an every-
thing-will-be-fine manner. Luckily, I knew better.

"Why do I get the feeling that it's the door at the
end of the hall?" Benjamin said as we got off of the
elevator on the fourth floor. The sound of "Jam
Tonight" was so loud that you'd think Freddie
Jackson was inside the apartment performing.

I held my index finger down firmly on the

doorbell, pressing once, twice, and then a double ring on the third time around before hearing someone inside yell out something about the door already being open.

I turned the knob and stepped inside. Instantaneously, my name was being thrown throughout points and corners of the room from the foyer all the way into the living room. My popularity made me feel like I was up next to entertain, after Freddie that is. I waved, I smiled, we kept moving along. Benjamin did as I did. We continued to walk along, when George grabbed me up and insisted that I dance one with him.

"Girl, I'm your Uncle! You don't wave and pass by me like that!" Benjamin was laughing, urging me on.

"No, Uncle George! Later! I promise! Have you seen my mother?"

"Look in the kitchen!" he said, spinning around and around. I sure hoped he didn't fall out.

"Alright now girl, I'm gonna hold you to it! I see you witcha' boyfriend here. You don't have to introduce me if you don't want to, because I can introduce myself."

Benjamin laughed and said, "I'm Benjamin. It's good to meet you sir."

"I'm Willie, I've been knowing this child since she was a itty, bitty, baby." He raised his hands to his knee level, showing Benjamin just how high I was. "She can't play cute with me, I'll take her out!" Uncle George said forming a fist.

I knew that he'd had one too many beers. In this case it was best to let him have his say, or he'd never stop talking.

"I'll take you out too young fella! If you don't treat my niece right," he said.

"Yes sir," Benjamin answered, as I took his hand and led him further into the crowd en route to the kitchen.

I pushed the kitchen door open to see one of my aunts and Cuz bustling around inside. Pots were being scrubbed, dishes were being washed, and remnants of food leftovers were being put away into plastic containers. I gave Benjamin's hand a gentle squeeze and said,

"Ma, we're here."

"And what would you like for me to do, Leslie? Roll out the red carpet for you?" Her tone was short and sarcastic, just like the temper I'd genetically inherited from her. She reached under the cabinet to put the heavy black iron skillet back into its place.

"Cuz! Hey!" Rachelle said, greeting me with a warm hug. I couldn't help but to look over at my mother as Rachelle hugged me.

"Benjamin, right? Welcome to the family. It's good to finally meet you," she said, giving him a hug, too. Go Cuz, I thought to myself. That family thing would win high praises with me later on. You know, people say that my mother and I can pass for sisters, we favor so much. It's strictly external, inside we're nothing alike. Look at her, she won't even stop for a minute to acknowledge my presence. Putting away the pots and clearing the countertops, that's what's most important.

"Ma, there's someone that I'd like for you to meet," I said moving in closer to where she was standing. If it had been left up to me, I'd have gone the other way.

"Leslie, don't you see me in the middle of something?"

"I'm Benjamin, and it's a pleasure to finally meet you Ms. Williams," Benjamin said, coming right over to her, and introducing himself. It was a good thing he had. I would have probably stormed out of that house if he hadn't. My patience was starting to wear thin.

"Well it's nice to meet you too, Benjamin," my mother said. "Leslie brought you over here so late. You've practically missed all the food."

"It's okay Ms. Williams, I. . . ."

I shot Benjamin a look.

"I'd be glad to have whatever's leftover," he said, correcting his answer just in the nick of time.

My mother went over to the microwave and popped out a hot plate with the works on it. There was turkey, greens, turnips, macaroni, candied sweets, I thought she said he'd missed all the food.

Benjamin looked over at me as if to say, how am I gonna eat all of this?

"Thank you Ms. Williams," he said, as he took a seat at the kitchen table.

"There wouldn't happen to be a plate in there for me now would there, Ma?" My mother sucked her teeth, eventually giving a nod yes, going on with her work and chatting along with my two aunts.

"Thumbs up, Leslie."

"Where are the kids?"

"In the room with the others playing Sega Genesis of course," Rachelle said, after pulling me off to the side.

"Of course," I answered. "Thanks for the thumbs up. I think Ma is warming up to him, too," I said as I looked over at Benjamin eating the food my mother had prepared for him. It certainly didn't look like he was having any trouble eating two Thanksgiving meals.

I warmed up my plate and took a seat next to Benjamin at the round wood table with the silver metal legs that I'd known since I was a child. I hated that old thing, but my mother just refused to get rid of it. I offered to buy her one of those new modern glass table dining sets for Christmas last year but she refused. She told me that if I went ahead and bought it, that she'd give it away to Goodwill.

My first bite of food told me in no unspoken words that there was no food like your Mama's.

"Benjamin, would you like to have a slice of double-layer chocolate cake?" Ma offered.

"No thank you, Ms. Williams, I couldn't eat another bite right this second, but I'd be glad to have it to take home."

"Well I can't make you no promises, but I'll try to put a piece on the side for you. Now how old did you say you were?" my mother asked.

"I didn't say, Ms. Williams, but I'm 35."

"And how many kids?"

"Just one," he answered.

I looked at Cuz, who looked over at the wall. I hated this question-and-answer shit.

"You're not married, are you?"

"No, Ms. Williams, I've been divorced for 5 years now, but don't worry, if I marry your daughter her uncle has already volunteered to take me out if I mistreat her."

"Ma, enough with the questions already," I told her.

"Leslie, nobody's talking to you, and you watch your tone," she said laughing at what Benjamin had just said.

It's fine, I told myself. She's allowed to have a moment. I've got all the respect in the world for my mother, and if she says watch my tone, then you better believe that I'm watching it. I knew that she wouldn't think twice about slapping me silly in front of everybody. That's right, even at the age of 21.

Benjamin was doing good so far, especially under this pressure. I hoped he didn't tell too much. Too much was the fact that he still lives with another woman, too much was the fact that he was my first, and too much was the fact that we'd stopped at his brother's before we came here.

"So why were you all so late?" my mother asked. She came over to the table with a sponge, wiping it down with clean even strokes, as both Benjamin and myself still sat around it.

"Car trouble, Ms. Williams. The engine went out on us."

Yeah, the engine went out on us alright, right in front of his brother Vernon's house.

"Make sure that doesn't happen again, baby. You might want to consider purchasing a new one. In this family, we like to sit down and eat together. Leslie knows better."

"Okay, Ms. Williams," Benjamin said giving me a wink.

"Call me Joan," she said. My baby had done real good, real good. I looked over at Benjamin, then back over at Cuz. We shared a smile between the three of us.

fair lady

He's not here yet."

"And I know I'm not going," Rachelle said to me over the line in a matter-of-fact tone.

"Wait, what are you talking about? You're not going where with who?" I asked as I paced up and down the floor of my livingroom.

"I'm not going with Nathaniel to dinner."

"Who's Nathaniel?" I asked.

"Nathaniel Wallace, will you keep up with me already? Nathaniel is the church guy. He's the bald-headed cutie."

"So then why aren't you going?"

"Instincts. My instincts are telling me not to show."

"Your instincts are telling you not to go out on

a date with a bald-headed cutie church guy named Nathaniel Wallace? He's already in the church, what've you got to lose?" I laughed.

"Church does not equal free of sin or lustful desire, Leslie."

"So why don't you two get together and pray for strength until after the ceremony?"

"You don't understand, Leslie."

"Yes I do, you agreed to go out with him. You're just not gonna show up."

"Right. He got my telephone number from his aunt. He called me and asked me out, and I said yes. It's kinda like a shame, because I'm dressed and everything, but I'm still not going."

"Well it's your call, Cuz, and it is only dinner. Nobody can make you do anything that you don't want to do. I personally fail to see the logic behind your reasoning. I mean, you haven't even given him a chance to mess up," I told her.

"Why are you breathing so hard?" Rachelle asked me, changing the subject. "Leslie, are you pacing?"

"Yes I am, thought you'd never notice," I said, falling out onto the sofa with my legs crossed, but shaking sporadically. "The whole time that you were talking I wanted to scream out, what about me?" I said.

"You couldn't get any more self absorbed could you? What, is it Benjamin? I really like him for you. And you know you were right. He was a hit on Thanksgiving."

"He's not here yet," I said in an emotionless tone. It hadn't mattered either way to me if he had been a hit on Thanksgiving or not. The point was that he was not here, with me, now. When he was supposed to be.

"So he's late! Why don't you give that man a break?" Rachelle said as she slipped off the dress she wore, skillfully placing it on its hanger.

"You don't get it. He's late. Over 4 hours!"

"Did he call?"

"No call whatsoever."

"Well is it like him? I've never heard you complain about this before."

"A few times. He hasn't shown. But he does usually call."

"Well maybe he got caught up with something at work."

"Or just maybe he's with her."

"Don't go there Leslie," Rachelle said.

"Why shouldn't I? What am I supposed to do, deny the woman's total existence altogether? Am I supposed to not wonder where he is and what he's doing when I can't lay a hand on him, when he's working, or not with me? It's like, I keep waiting for that phone call from him, the phone call where he tells me that it's all over between us. It's the phone call where I find out that our relationship wasn't worth the risk, the risk of losing what he has with her and his son." I could feel the numbness make its way through my legs, which I'd just stopped shaking.

"Leslie, you need to calm down. This relationship is taking a bigger toll on you than you think. Why don't you talk to him? So he doesn't show, he doesn't call. The question is what are you gonna do about it?"

"What am I gonna do about it? Well, first thing tomorrow morning, I'm gonna march myself right on over to where he's working. Then I'm gonna tell him how upset I was that he stood me up. Then I'm gonna ask him what he plans to do about his living situation. If I don't like what he's saying, it's over for me, case closed," I said, in an adamant tone with a sistagirl roll of my eyes. It meant I was serious about what I'd just said.

❖

"Hey, what are you doing here?" Benjamin asked me, as he held a large beam up, drilling the silver nail into its place on the wall.

"We need to talk," I told him, as his workmen passed back and forth between us. "Privately," I made sure to add.

We walked into an empty room in the back filled with supplies of joint compound, more wood beams, redbrick, and plaster.

"So what happened yesterday? You never

showed up, you never called. I thought we had plans."

"I'm sorry honey. My son got sick. He had a fever of 101, he couldn't keep anything down. I was up with him for most of the night. I didn't get to sleep at all."

"Well is he alright?" I asked. Suddenly, it hadn't seemed all that bad to have been stood up. His son being the reason. There I was worrying over nothing. Well I wouldn't say nothing. Anything, as long as it wasn't her.

"Benjamin, I've been thinking a lot lately. And I think it's time you made a decision about us."

"Leslie, I already told you I want us," he said taking one of my hands into his.

"No, that's not what I mean. I'm talking about your living situation. I'm talking about this constant back-and-forth thing you're doing," I said, releasing his grip on my hand.

Benjamin heaved a heavy sigh and answered, "You're right, I need to make a decision. I understand where you're coming from, and I know that it's not fair to you."

"It's not fair to anyone Benjamin. Not to me or Sonia for that matter. It's probably only fair to you."

"What do you mean by that?" he asked.

"I mean that you get to have your cake, and eat it too."

"I disagree."

"Really? How so?" I asked inquisitively, with widened eyes and opened ears.

"I just disagree, that's all," he answered. "It's not as easy as you think it is. But I will make a decision, if that's what you want. Can you give me until next Friday?"

It had only been Tuesday. Ten days to wait on what could be a hurdle in the milestone of my future. *Ten days*. An acceptance of the equivalent of 240 measly hours that would give him the power I so struggled to sustain. The power of my own self-worth.

"Yes, I'll give you until Friday, Benjamin."

"Do you want to do something later?" he asked me as I began to walk towards the door, leaving the room.

"No, I think it's better that I just see you next week," I said, thinking I'd better call Cuz and ask her to put an extra prayer in for me on this one.

coming 'round the mountain

We want to thank you all for coming out to Holy Christian Faith Temple this morning on this special Pray for Someone Special Sunday. As Christians, we sometimes lose sight of what's important. It's not about the fish fries, or the bouncing gospel choirs, or even the aesthetics of the temple we reside in. To be about these things is a breeding ground for hierarchy, and a distraction of our focus. Our focus, ladies and gentlemen, should always be on the word." Pastor Holmes' voice echoed, and when he stretched out his arms, his black and gold robe flared out like wings of an eagle. "It's about fellowshiping," he continued, "and it's about unselfishness, thinking of others who might be less fortunate than ourselves. We are asking you to come forward and say a silent prayer for that special person in your life. They could be sick, maybe they just lost their job and the rent is due and the bills are starting to pile up, maybe they've got a secret drug habit that no one knows about except you. It's about being unselfish, please come forward now."

Rachelle slowly walked up towards the front of the church, where Pastor Holmes, a deacon, and a handful of parishioners were, all on bended knee. She could hear the muffled sobs and the praises of the Thank You Fathers. Would it be alright? At home was one thing, but to go up and pray for Leslie's happiness? To pray that Benjamin made the decision to leave his family to be with her cousin? She'd sounded so sad that night as she told her the story of what had happened. Benjamin made her so happy. This prayer was for all the right reasons, it wasn't for her. This one was for Leslie. Rachelle joined the rest of the parishioners at the front of the pulpit, knelt down, closed her eyes, and began to pray, hard. Then something happened, Rachelle opened her mouth to utter a word of praise only to feel the taste of salt on the tip of her tongue. Water was streaming down her face, and wouldn't stop. "Thank you God, oh thank you!" A feeling of newness took its home inside of Rachelle's body, causing it to spasm, and shake so that Pastor Holmes and another male church member had to come over and make sure that she didn't hurt herself. "Thank you Lord! Thank you!" Rachelle kept repeating and shaking, and crying. The feeling was slowing down enough for Rachelle to be aware of her surroundings, and the people around her. "Pastor Holmes," she slowly spoke, "I'm ready."

"Are you sure Sister Rachelle?"

"I am."

"Are you ready to join the extended family of God?"

"I am!" Rachelle said once more, in a strong self-assured tone.

Rachelle had gotten saved, and it was right. She could feel it. The Lord was blessing her, even when she had tried to pray for another.

"Congratulations Sister Rachelle," a voice had said. Everyone in the church had been hugging her and when she turned around to see where the voice was coming from she was pleasantly surprised.

"Nathaniel," she said, wiping her face of the tears of happiness that just seemed to keep coming. "I must look a mess."

"Actually, you've never looked prettier. Don't I get a hug?" Nathaniel asked holding his arms open.

"Of course you do," Rachelle answered with a big smile.

"Welcome to the family."

"What? When did you?"

"Mid-week service, I felt it was time, it felt . . ."

"Right?" Rachelle said, finishing Nathaniel's sentence.

"Very."

"Listen Nathaniel, I'm sorry about the other night," she said, taking his hand in hers and going to sit down at the bench.

"I understand, I didn't want you to feel pressured."

"It was only dinner," Rachelle said in an embarrassed tone.

"I think it meant a little more than that to you."

"It did, just being married and divorced, then dating around. I finally found someone who I'm sure that I want to be with for the rest of my life. I didn't want to jeopardize that with anything worldly. But I realize now, that if I continue to put Him first, that I'm gonna be alright."

"That's right. And the man for you won't ask to go before God."

"Now what?" Rachelle looked up at Nathaniel and asked.

"Now," Nathaniel said, taking ahold of Rachelle's hand, "I ask you, if you'll consider putting me second in your life." One single tear streamed down the front of Nathaniel's face.

Some might take tears as a sign of weakness in a man, but from where I'm sitting now, it's an outright sign of strength.

"Is that a marriage proposal?" Rachelle asked in her Sista tone.

"No," Nathaniel laughed, "I'm saying, we

hardly know each other, but I'd like to get the chance to."

"Okay," Rachelle answered back with a smile. Nathaniel leaned in to give her a hug and Rachelle closed her eyes once again. Mmhmm, that's right. "Thank you, Jesus."

severed ties

T·hat thing I did, I know it's called an ultima-
tum. My terms make it an all-or-nothing
deal. *Those things never work*. There's supposed
to be one more day before Benjamin comes to me
with his answer. *Couldn't wait. Thursday is about
as good as it's gonna get.* Now I've gone on ahead
and called him, moving it up 24 hours. I just had
to, I'm totally in love with the man. What had I
been thinking? I smoothed over my turquoise
satin top and had just lined my mouth with the
new plum lipstick I purchased yesterday when
the doorbell rings. It's him, it's him. I suddenly
feel like a child because I'm all giddy and nervous.

"Leslie, I missed you so much," Benjamin said,
giving me the biggest hug and kiss ever.

"Benjamin."

"You look good."

"It's only been a couple of days," I said.

"I know, but that's even more of a reason to tell you what I have to say," he said walking me into the livingroom.

"No, wait. Me first," I told him as I sat across from him.

"Leslie I want us," Benjamin interrupted. "The truth is that I didn't plan on getting into a relationship with you. It did start out as a challenge, but I fell for the person you are. I love your strengths, and your enthusiasm, but most of all, I love you. I've left Sonia and I had a long talk with my son. He knows that I'm always gonna be there for him. I'm staying in my apartment building in the Bronx. Sonia says that she doesn't agree with my decision, but that she also doesn't want to be with someone who doesn't want to be with her."

All the while that Benjamin is talking, I'm seeing something. I'm hearing and seeing at the same time. I guess my mother's right. I do think too much. I see ... *Benjamin coming into the house at some ungodly hour and I'm asking him where he's been and who he's been with. It happens on a regular basis, so much so that I'm spending my every waking moment wondering the same thing all the time. Where were you at and who were you with? It's all I want to know. Yeah, I'm down with the Po-lice. Leslie-Patrol. It's why I'm the one asking all the questions.*

I stay sexy, I try being the intellectual, and I'm still my own individual, but I'm not the same. I'm changing, only for the worse. I was waiting for him to make a change when he wasn't with me, and the sad news is that I still am, even living together under the same roof. Our relationship is nothing like the way I pictured it, namely because Sonia put up with the things that I can't. I never thought that the space he said he needed would be between us.

"Benjamin, you didn't let me finish," I said standing up. "I just can't. It's gonna take more than being in love to get through this. The love does count for a lot. It's important for you to know that it's mutual and that I don't have any regrets about meeting you, or what we had. If I could make one wish and have it come true, it would be that we could only go on . . ."

"But it can Leslie."

"How?" I looked around my livingroom, making the dried floral rose bouquet that Benjamin had given me my focal point. He sat on the edge of the couch and stood there looking at those flowers too. There was at least ten minutes worth of silence. "I wouldn't have had to push you to leave if you wanted to," I said softly. "I wouldn't even have had to say a word. It would just be done. It can only mean one thing . . . That you're unsure yourself.

"Benjamin, I can be sure for me.

"I can be sure that I'll get up in the morning and brush my teeth.

"I can be sure that I'll give my career the best that I've got.

"I can be sure that I learn something new every day.

"But I can't be sure for you.

"I can't spend my life trying to make you sure that you made the right decision in leaving. It's something that you need to know yourself."

Benjamin sighed, "You're right. I'm not sure, but I don't want to lose you."

"And I don't want to lose you, but it's not fair for you to have me holding on to a what if. I can only offer you my friendship, platonic because we both know that sex will only complicate things further," I chuckled. "But who knows?"

"This isn't over, Leslie. I'm going to prove that you're all the woman I need in my life," Benjamin had said on his way out the door.

❖

Busy, busy, busy. That's me. It looks like my building's gonna make it to the next level in the program after all. Mr. Hill finally pitched in and helped me to take up the slack. Our repair plan has been approved and the first thing that they're gonna fix is that damn elevator. Yes, there is one. And I got that ABC internship. I'll be working for World News Tonight. I start in two weeks, and I can't wait. It also seems as though I'll be the one helping to plan a wedding because Patrice is getting married to Lance, the chef. She's talking about getting married on a boat. Lance can't swim, and she wants to be sure that this one doesn't get away. Rachelle doesn't have the same problem. Her new boyfriend is oh so in love with her and the kids. I like Nathaniel, he's just what Cuz needs. He told me that he's planning on surprising her with an engagement ring on Christmas Day.

And my love life? Well for now there is none, but I do know that there's somebody out there who loves me, and I will probably always love him.

Check these sizzlers
from sisters who deliver!

SKIN DEEP
BY KATHLEEN CROSS   0-380-81130-8/$6.99 US/$8.99 CAN

HOMECOURT ADVANTAGE
BY RITA EWING AND CRYSTAL McCRARY
                        0-380-79901-4/$6.99 US/$8.99 CAN

SHOE'S ON THE OTHA' FOOT
BY HUNTER HAYES   0-06-101466-4/$6.50 US/$8.99 CAN

WISHIN' ON A STAR
BY EBONI SNOE   0-380-81395-5/$5.99 US/$7.99 CAN

A CHANCE ON LOVIN' YOU
BY EBONI SNOE   0-380-79563-9/$5.99 US/$7.99 CAN

TELL ME I'M DREAMIN'
BY EBONI SNOE   0-380-79562-0/$5.99 US/$7.99 CAN

AIN'T NOBODY'S BUSINESS IF I DO
BY VALERIE WILSON WESLEY
                        0-380-80304-6/$6.99 US/$9.99 CAN

IF YOU WANT ME
BY KAYLA PERRIN   0-380-81378-5/$5.99 US/$7.99 CAN
